LOOKING FOR JOAN
AND OTHER STORIES

ALSO PUBLISHED BY TROUBADOR

AMERICA AWAITS US, MY LOVELY and Other Stories

'Beautifully written and really evocative of a particular time and place'
Emily Trahair, Editor, *Planet Magazine*

LOOKING FOR JOAN
AND OTHER STORIES

Christopher Owen

Copyright © 2024 Christopher Owen

The moral right of the author has been asserted.

Apart from any fair dealing for the purposes of research or private study, or criticism or review, as permitted under the Copyright, Designs and Patents Act 1988, this publication may only be reproduced, stored or transmitted, in any form or by any means, with the prior permission in writing of the publishers, or in the case of reprographic reproduction in accordance with the terms of licences issued by the Copyright Licensing Agency. Enquiries concerning reproduction outside those terms should be sent to the publishers.

This is a work of fiction. Names, characters, businesses, places, events and incidents are either the products of the author's imagination or used in a fictitious manner. Any resemblance to actual persons, living or dead, or actual events is purely coincidental.

Troubador Publishing Ltd
Unit E2 Airfield Business Park,
Harrison Road, Market Harborough,
Leicestershire LE16 7UL
Tel: 0116 279 2299
Email: books@troubador.co.uk
Web: www.troubador.co.uk

ISBN 978-1-80514-262-1

British Library Cataloguing in Publication Data.
A catalogue record for this book is available from the British Library.

Printed and bound in the UK by TJ Books Limited, Padstow, Cornwall
Typeset in 11pt Minion Pro by Troubador Publishing Ltd, Leicester, UK

For Joy

CONTENTS

Misconnections	1
Changing Places	25
The Bar on the Third Floor	38
Cyril, Eyes Full of Drink	46
A Day at the Cricket	57
Kings Cross	76
Stranded in Bristol	84
The Park	98
Jack	108
That's All Right, She Says	114
Carrie's Story	120
A Portrait	128
Across the Fields	137
The Song of the Widow, Mrs Williams of South Road, Crosby	138
The Accident	152
Pig's Knuckle, New York	159
Fabrics	161
Looking for Joan	162
In the Beginning	171

MISCONNECTIONS

Adrian and **Susie**, in their flat in Maida Vale, North London, were yelling and screaming at each other at two in the morning when their front door bell rang. Exhausted and unable to master their thoughts, they opened the door to discover their neighbour who lived in the flat below them, a woman who on a number of occasions had complained about the noise, standing on the threshold seething with rage and brandishing a kitchen knife.

Thereafter, there had been a change, in that they no longer yelled and threw things but communicated with each other with, for the most part, feigned politeness and restraint.

She and Adrian had first met when he was a professor of Imperial History at Bristol, and she was teaching English Literature at a nearby further education college. She thought him just wonderful at the time. They had been full of hopes. It was the River Avon, she believed, that had cemented their relationship, with their walks along its banks, and their visits to The Hatchet Inn in Frogmore Street, both of them drinking pints of best bitter. Their long discussions, feminism, Marx. They had been reading from the same page. He had said so. Had used those very words. 'We're reading from the same page,' he had said, with that nod of his. In those early days she had been all up-in-the-air, bright as a bird, arms waving, all elbows.

And he was charming in his own way. Up for a good time. Pretty good in bed, she had to admit.

Now, and for too long, he had not been the same man; his features, the whole lot of him, had deteriorated. He had become sceptical and apprehensive, spending much of his day in his study, reading and writing copious notes on Nineteenth Century political history, surrounded by what he professed to love, the dark Victorian wallpaper, his books, and eighteenth and nineteenth century prints and antique clocks, that gave him an impression of himself as he was, a university educated intellectual. Through thick and thin, he cleaved to and was sustained by the steady slow pace of his life.

He was a man of intellect, an academic, in prolonged and certain grief for a broken first marriage of long ago.

'My wife Delia and I were too young,' he had told Susie. 'The pub, coming home late. Incompatible,' he had said.

Adrian was peeping round the kitchen doorway now. He was anxious that Susie, who was helping herself to another glass of gin from the bottle on the kitchen counter, would suddenly turn around and catch him spying on her in his worried way.

He wondered again how Susie had arrived at such 'a disappointing state of dissipation'. Frankly, for all the concern he had for her, he couldn't in all honesty say he liked her. Not for a long time. Her red lips – now hidden from his view, she with her back to him – used to be full and inviting. But in recent times they had appeared to him as a red wound, the consequence of some misbegotten malpractice. She had, no doubt about it, let herself go.

She knew he was there. He'd been there before, spying on her, not knowing what to say, but only, in his own mind, having it confirmed that sadly she was an incurable drunkard. To her way of thinking, it wasn't the least surprising that she drank.

'I can see you,' she said.

'Ah,' he said.

He determined to confront the situation and attempted to step into the kitchen. But when he tried to do so, he felt a sharp pain in his lower back. He couldn't move.

'Are you still here?' she asked without turning to him.

'I'm stuck,' he said. 'May have twisted something.'

'Oh dear.'

She could have another gin if only he'd buzz off, she thought. She considered retiring to her bedroom to watch Death in Paradise on television. But to leave the kitchen she'd have had to try to squeeze past him and it would have resulted in her having to touch his body with hers.

She made to approach him, then changed her mind and returned to the safety of the gin bottle on the kitchen counter.

He made another attempt to straighten up. But he couldn't.

Earlier that year she had secretly booked into a private hospital and had had a face lift. She had recently been seeing a man in the motor trade who was twenty years younger than she. The surgical procedure was supposed to have been a surprise, a gift for him. But when he saw what she had done, he had been disappointed. He had told her he had always preferred older women.

Adrian felt he couldn't very well stay in the kitchen doorway all day and all night. He had to persuade her to cooperate.

'The gin looks good,' he said. 'Quite fancy a drop or two myself.'

'Wouldn't you prefer a beer?' she said.

'No, no. A gin would go down very nicely, I would say.'

'There's beer in the fridge,' she said.

'No. Gin. Let it be gin, dear,' he said.

He had called her 'dear'. He's panicking, she thought.

'Just a wee drop,' he said.

Now he'd gone all Scottish on her, she observed. This was new anyway. She poured herself another gin. And then she poured him a glass equivalent to two tots. She walked unsteadily towards him. Stretched out an arm and placed the glass in his left hand.

'Bottoms up,' she said as she returned to the bottle on the kitchen counter.

He looked at his glass.

'Drink up,' she said to him, without turning.

'Very nice. Didn't think I'd like it. But I do. I do. No tonic, I suppose?'

'No.'

'Oh, that's a generous measure,' he said, after she had again topped up his glass.

'I've another bottle at the back of the bread bin,' she said.

'Mm. Tasty,' he said.

He imbibed a large mouthful, winced and swallowed.

She returned to him with the new bottle.

As she did so, he again attempted to straighten himself, but nothing budged.

'You could give me a push,' he said.

'Well, let's have a go,' she said.

Holding her glass in one hand, with the other she gave him a push, but in doing so, lost balance and fell backwards onto the kitchen floor.

'Are you alright?' he asked her.

He looked down and there she was, her wide red lips open, and he thought, as far as he could now think, the gin having got the better of him, how her lying there with her wide red mouth reminded him of those halcyon days, oh, so many years ago, when she and he had kissed beneath the tree in St James' Park, how she had giggled as she was doing now, and how the same giggle, the same red mouth, her skinny frame had caught him in a net of affection, how they had, the two of them, made love in the evening after he had returned home from playing at wicket for Brondesbury Road Cricket Club.

'Gin,' she called.

It took several minutes for her to scramble to her feet. She leaned against the doorpost, swayed backwards to gain all the strength she could and launched herself at him, causing him at first to straighten, then fall backwards into the hallway, and she followed him, her body crashing heavily onto his.

Half the night they lay there, and on waking, it became apparent that their life together, their marriage, seemed to have been revived and re-established in that they found they were relatively at ease with each other, a benign condition that continued throughout much of the day. During the afternoon departing from their usual routine they watched A Streetcar Named Desire on television, both agreeing the actress Joan Blandingford was absolutely wonderful as Blanche DuBois.

'She's amazing, so vulnerable,' Susie said. 'It's so sad about her.'

After the film there was even a brief moment when the possibility of sex hung in the air.

Late that evening, Susie quietly and for a brief while stood at Adrian's study door, as he, his back towards her, was leaning over his books. As was his habit, he was tunelessly and irritatingly humming the first movement of Beethoven's Eroica Symphony No. 3 in E flat major.

After a moment she returned to the bottle of dry gin on the kitchen counter.

Susie and Adrian split up the following summer. Adrian sold the flat and went to stay in Bristol, half a mile from where his first wife Delia lived with her husband Barry and their two teenage boys. He had earlier suggested to Delia that he might move to Bristol, and she had pointedly told him she thought it a bad idea. She declined to expand on that statement. If he couldn't see the disadvantages, indeed the folly of his proposed action, there was, in her view, little point in her trying to explain them to him.

*

Delia and Barry may not have had the most perfect of marriages, but one had to do the best one could she told her reflection in the bathroom mirror as she brushed and flossed her teeth in the mornings after breakfast. Teeth were important to Delia. Hers were frequently admired by people, both male and female and this reassured her, although from time to time it had left her wondering why no other part of her, her hair, for instance, or her eyes which were an olive green, had ever received the selfsame appreciation.

Since her divorce from Adrian in the late 1990's, and before marrying Barry four years ago, Delia had been living off and on, more off than on, with Lennox, a Scottish painter and decorator with an explosive temper, who had gone to live in Spain. She could have joined him. The invitation, however duplicitous, had been there, but she had declined to do so.

Her husband Barry worked in the city centre. What he did there Delia was not able to ascertain, not in any detail, something to do with investments and hedge funding, all of which was quite beyond her. But after Lennox, she found Barry properly dependable, or more precisely she thought him unexceptionable and generally unexciting, or was the word 'tolerable'? It was frustrating that she was unable to find the right word or words for him. For someone like her who was intent on writing a novel, it was frustrating to find that she had to consult Thesaurus on Google so frequently. In the end she had settled on Barry being 'disappointing'. She wouldn't want it known to others, but sex with Barry was to her no more than him 'sticking his thing' into her, after which short-lived event he would rise from her bed, and posing before the bedroom mirror would proceed to thump his chest like Tarzan of the Apes and subsequently would throw back his head and bellow Johnny Weissmuller's ululating Jungle call, This caused Delia, lying on her back in the bed, the sheet pulled up to her chin, to worry lest the neighbours, Mr and Mrs Blackstone and their Alsatian would begin to bang on the adjoining wall. Even so, the fact was, Delia needed security, which with Adrian and then Lennox had been missing. So, Barry remained in situ. She thought 'in situ' a neat turn of phrase.

It had been her own literary ambitions that had attracted her to Adrian all those years ago. He was a man of words, of that there was no manner of doubt, 'no manner of doubt whatever'. She loved Gilbert and Sullivan and when irked by something or someone, when feeling put out, out of sorts, on edge, she'd hum and sing along to herself from their comic operettas. Adrian had loved G&S as well. That was to say when he was at home and not at work or the pub. It had been the pub, him with his pals which was the final straw. He became morose, unbearably restless, and on occasion unexpectedly violent, although the recipients of his drunken outbursts had been mostly the kitchen crockery. Then there had been the front door which he had attempted to break down after she had changed the locks. He had become no longer the man she had married. Or maybe, she had surmised, it had been that she had failed to recognize the man he was, and had married him while mistakenly thinking he was someone else. It had been all too ghastly. Fortunately, things being as they were, they hadn't had children.

If she were truthful, that was to say honest with herself, she'd have to admit that she hadn't had much luck with men. But then, as she had come to understand from other women, it was unlikely she would ever meet a man who was altogether satisfactory, who was entirely capable of maintaining a mutually satisfying heterosexual relationship.

Delia's difficulty in choosing the words and phrases with which to express herself had been exacerbated once she had joined the creative writing group run by Felicity Manning in her Grade 2 listed Regency family home in the leafy Bristol suburb of Cotham.

There were eight and sometimes nine members of the group, not including Felicity, that number having shrunk from the fourteen who had attended when the group had been formed the previous year. Of the few members Delia knew by name was a middle-aged woman called Rose who, despite the unusually hot weather that summer, was never seen to take off her coat. Then there was a thin stick of a woman of formidable opinions called Janet, and Dick, a professorial type in his late sixties, who was a student counsellor at a local college of education, who said he was writing a thesis on

'Myth in Classical Athens, Identity, Ideology and Experience', and who, Delia suspected, wary of being the only man in the company of women those Friday afternoons in Cotham, took an unnervingly long time to say whatever it was he wanted to say, much of which was beyond Delia's understanding. Of those attending, however, it was Dick whom Delia liked the most.

Felicity herself naturally chaired the proceedings, intent of keeping the peace and making everyone comfortable, which at times proved an uphill task. Delia was to discover there were rules regarding what one could and what one could not write or say. These rules were promulgated and insisted upon by the member called Janet, who, on the afternoon Delia had first attended a group meeting, had informed Delia that she, being a white woman, would have to be extra careful should she decide to include a person of colour in her narrative. Not that Delia had intended to do such a thing. Janet was eager to alert everyone in advance to the linguistic dangers of the day. Words to be avoided would include basket case, long time no see, first class, fall on deaf ears, and mankind. The list was seemingly unending and left Delia feeling perplexed. It was made clear to her by Janet, that should she wish to secure a publisher for her forthcoming book she would have to be absolutely sure the work in question complied with the regulations. 'It's all a bit Stalinist, isn't it?' Delia had said, which observation Janet had immediately interpretated as a personal attack on herself. 'It's nothing of the sort,' She had snapped, and muttering that she had just remembered she had an urgent appointment, had left the meeting, only to return the following week fully rearmed.

Soon after joining, it struck Delia that Felicity, the founder and chair-person, had no sense of humour. She appeared to struggle to understand and appreciate a joke or humourous remark that any member of the group might proffer. She made it clear that she felt deeply about other people's misfortunes, their domestic upsets, difficult births, unstable marriages, their 'passing', and did so with furrowed brow. She was forever urging those attending to sign petitions in protest against victimisation, evidence of which she saw everywhere. No one was safe from her compassion. She spoke against and confronted inhumanity to animals, and the plight of refugees. It seemed to Delia that Felicity would be profoundly disturbed whatever the cause. Crack a joke, on the other hand, make a half-humorous remark and she would stare back at one in blank and anxious incomprehension.

*

Adrian was on his own now, had been for the six months since he and Susie had parted company. He had rented a flat in Bristol, where, quite by chance, he bumped into Larna, an old flame from when they were undergraduates.

'It was quite miraculous, quite extraordinary,' he told Delia when he and Delia met for lunch at The Bristol Harbour Hotel.

All those years, he and Larna never once seeing each other and then she pops up at the Farmer's Market on Whiteladies Road. She was buying a leek. This bloody big leek and she had waved it at him. Astonishing. It was as if it were only yesterday. They'd gone for a cup of tea, he told Delia. At a local tea shop. It had been like old times. Only she was married and with teenage kids. Boy and a girl.

He was, in meeting Delia, in paying for her salad, orange chocolate mousse and cappuccino, seeking her advice. Her reassurance, if it were possible.

'You've messed up enough marriages already,' she said.

'You and I were too young,' he said.

'You and Susie.'

'We weren't married.'

'Same difference,' she said. She thought that 'same difference' would fit the bill, that it wasn't one of those phrases that was no longer acceptable.

'What am I to do?' he asked.

It was a bloody cheek, she thought, him moving to within a couple of miles of where she and Barry lived. He hadn't met Barry. Not as yet, and she wasn't at all keen for them to meet. Barry was Barry, and Adrian was Adrian and they were 'chalk and cheese'. And what was wrong with a cliche if it worked, she told herself. Bloody Janet at those Friday meetings, she thought.

'You must do what you feel best,' she said to Adrian.

'But I don't know what is best,' he said. 'I passed your house the other day,' he said. 'Late Victorian. 1890's I'd say. The terracotta detailing. Actually, not so different from the house we had in Chidder Road.'

He was getting personal now. He would be inviting himself to dinner in less than no time, she thought. Forget it.

'You're smiling,' he said. 'What's the joke? Love your smile. Terrific. Always said so.'

'Best bit of me,' she said.

'Well, I only know everyone we knew thought your smile, your bright white teeth were enchanting.'

'I have to go,' she said. 'My husband, Barry is expecting me. We're going to watch the cricket on the BBC.'

Barry loved cricket. She didn't. But she had to say something.

'I'll see you home,' Adrian said.

'No, no. Please. I can manage,' she said.

Adrian was walking back to the flat he had rented while he looked for one that he could buy and that he felt would suit him. It had become so difficult, indeed quite impossible to replicate his and Susie's old flat in London. He had come to realize just how much he loved that flat; his study, the sense of history, the bay windows, the bookcases which he had been obliged to leave behind, the Victorian fireplace, the cornicing, the rose in the ceiling centre. He had had to put all or nearly all his books in storage, along with the clocks, the pictures and various ornaments. It was heart breaking. He felt bereft. That was it, he was in grief, he thought now as he walked down Corn Street. He was cast out. On his own. It could have worked out, somehow or other with Susie, although she became impossible. All the drinking. He could be back home, taking the Tube to the London Library, to the Imperial War Museum, the V&A. He ought not to have left. He could have bought or rented a place near to where they had lived in Maida Vale. He had tried to do so. He had given it a go. But he had felt at a loss, estranged. There he was in Bristol, living in the rented upstairs flat of a plain 1950's semidetached house and he, at that moment, as he was walking down Clare Street towards the city centre, was wondering why. Why he was living there. What the hell had he thought he was doing. There seemed to be no end to the situation.

As for Susie, he didn't know where she had got to. She'd just disappeared, which, to his mind, was inconsiderate. After all they'd been together, in all but name, as man and wife for years. They may have separated and perhaps a good thing too, but it didn't mean she needed to be so unavailable, so beyond reach. And the nature of her leaving. The way she had arrived at his study door, with two suitcases, and, she told him, a taxi waiting. And her words: 'I'm leaving you, Adrian.' And his: 'Shouldn't we talk about this?' Then hers again: 'No. We've done all that.' And off she went. Out of the front door. It oughtn't to have come as a surprise, but still it did. He had rung her sister in Edinburgh. She'd said, God, she didn't know where she was. They hadn't spoken for years.

Then there was Larna. She hadn't called or texted him. He had checked his phone every half hour. He had tried not to. He told himself to desist. And there he was, doing so again.

He thought he knew Bristol. But he must have taken a wrong turning. He was in the road where Delia lived.

He decided he'd walk past her house, have a quick look over at it, then retrace his steps. There were the terracotta details, the ornate gables, sliding sash and canted bay windows. No sign of Delia, or anyone. It was a quiet road. An elderly man cleaning his Volvo in his driveway said, 'Can I help you?' 'No, no, thanks, I know where I am,' Adrian replied.

*

Felicity Manning and the members of her writing group were assembled in Felicity's kitchen in her family home in Cotham.

'We have a new member joining us this afternoon,' Felicity said. 'Thank you so much for coming, Larna. Larna tells me she is writing a book.'

'I've not yet started,' Larna said.

'What's it about?' Janet asked.

'Well, I thought a writer,' Larna said.

'You'd do well to avoid writing fiction about writers,' Janet said, 'Publishers can't bear novels which do that. They go straight onto the slush pile.'

'Some of Rachel Cusk's novels are about writers,' Delia said.

'Rachel Cusk is exceptional,' Janet said.

What a haughty little shit, she is, Delia thought.

'Louise May Alcott's Little Women, that's about a writer, isn't it?' Rose said.

'Michael Chabon's Wonder boys,' Dick said. 'That's about a writer.'

'Philip Roth, Ghost Writer,' a man sitting on his own in an armchair by the French windows said.

'Those are established authors. But I have it on good authority publishers are sick of that sort of fiction nowadays,' Janet said.

'Well, I'm sure we all have to write that to which each of us is suited. It's such a personal thing, isn't it?' Felicity said.

'Actually,' Larna said, 'it isn't about a writer as such. It's about a man, an academic, a professor of Nineteenth Century politics.'

'Have you got a name for him?' Dick asked.

'Not yet.'

'Oh, I do hope he's going to have a name,' Rose said. 'I can't bear it when it's all he and she and one doesn't know who's who. It's all so confusing. Like that Cromwell novel by what's-her-name. Wonderful, I'm sure, but I had to give up on it. After fifty pages I was quite lost. And I hate being lost. I lost my way in John Lewis's on Tuesday, and it was terrifying, I thought I'll never get out of the bloody building. It was not unlike what I felt when I was reading that Cromwell book. At least in John Lewis there was someone I could ask for the way out. That's the thing about John Lewis, there's always someone somewhere there when you need them. Not like M&S. God, I went in there to buy a cardigan, and there wasn't sight or sound of an assistant anywhere. Never is. I thought at the time, I've always thought, this lot isn't going to last out much longer, and anyway I can never find clothes there that suit me. It's all for goodness-knows-who.'

'You could call him Adrian,' Delia said to Larna. 'The man in your book, the academic. Adrian.'

*

Delia and **Larna** were sitting at a table in Patisserie La Reine in Union Street.

'Thank you for agreeing to meet up,' Delia said to Larna.

She'd love to hear more about her book, she told her.

'Well, there's nothing much to tell at the moment,' Larna said as they sat over their tea. 'I've not written before, and I thought if I could join a creative writing group it might help, show me the way, so to speak.'

'You mentioned a man,' Delia said. 'I think you said it's about a man. Adrian, is that his name?'

'Well, no. It doesn't have to be. It was you who suggested Adrian,' Larna said.

'So I did. How strange. The name just came to me. I was married to a man by that name. It sounded a bit like him.'

'Ah,' Larna said.

Larna was afraid that she might be on dangerous ground.

'This man in your novel, is he married?' she asked.

'Well, I suppose he could be. He has an affair.'

'With you,' Delia suggested.

'Well, it's not me. It's fiction after all,' Larna said.

'Always use what you know. If you've had a relationship with someone, use it,' Delia said. 'There's this young student, and she meets this rather dishy young undergraduate and they have a wonderful affair.'

It was all there, Delia told her, the college, the pub they used to go to, the things they did. The sex. Larna ought not to shy away from the sex. She was sure she wouldn't have to make that up, she could use her own experience Was he violent? Did he get drunk, out at the pub with his ghastly men friends night after night, and not be home till some ungodly hour?

'Gosh,' Larna said. 'I reckon you ought to write it. You'd do it better than me.'

'I expect he'll turn out to be a shit,' Delia said.

*

Adrian sat in the low-ceilinged living room of his cheerless rented flat north of Bristol city centre. Larna hadn't called him. He ought never to have come to Bristol. It had been Delia of course. The idea of reacquainting himself with her. To start again, which he knew was ridiculous. That was his problem he thought. He had become irrational. No books, no research, no constraining structure. He was all at sea. Best to just bugger off back to London.

He drove to Maida Vale and booked into a hotel half a mile from his and Susie's old flat. The next day, and on the days following, he went to the London Library to continue with his research. By this, as intended, he delayed having to make decisions regarding where he might rent or buy and when he'd be able to retrieve his books and personal belongings, his clocks and prints from storage. He needed, he told himself, breathing space, time in which to recalibrate.

What he missed was conversation. He supposed that in recent times he hadn't been especially gregarious. But to have no one at all, whoever they might be, to talk to was debilitating. It threw himself on himself. He looked about him, in the library, on the bus to and from the library, walking along the streets, and he was strangely and uncomfortably conscious of what appeared to him to be the distance between himself and others, between him and his immediate environment, the shops, the office buildings. He felt alienated, they from him, him from them. So that, one afternoon in the London Library, he hadn't been discomforted by an elderly somewhat unkempt man coming over to where he was sitting and enquiring whether he had read Mythology: Timeless Tales of Gods and Heroes, 75th Anniversary Illustrated Edition, by Edith Hamilton. Adrian hadn't. It was a fascinating book, the man said. His name was Dick, he told Adrian in the library suite on the sixth floor where conversation between members was permitted. He'd come down from Bristol for the day, as he did once a month. He was a member, had been for many years, was writing a thesis on 'Myth in Classical Athens, Identity, Ideology and Experience'. He preferred to research in the library, as he didn't own a computer. He had thought of purchasing one, but he feared he hadn't the technical expertise to be able to successfully operate it. He was in his late sixties and preferred to write in long hand, and once he had written two or three thousand words, he'd type them on an old Remington he had had for over twenty years, although he had found it increasingly difficult to find replacement ribbons, and had tracked down half a dozen in a second-hand book shop in Bristol, which would keep him going until he needed to find more ribbons, which hopefully he would manage to do. He had at one time thought he'd take the plunge and purchase a computer and had, in fact, discovered that one could do so direct from India where they were much less expensive than those on sale in the UK or elsewhere. He had made enquiries and then it had somehow slipped his mind to proceed with this further. He'd found, he said, that his time was more than sufficiently occupied in writing his thesis, which he had been writing in the mornings for fourteen years. At about two o'clock each day, he said, he'd have a spot of lunch, a sandwich and a walk in St George's Park near where he lived, and then in the evenings he'd partake of a glass or two of red wine which one could purchase most reasonably from the lower shelves at Tesco's. On Saturday afternoons when showing, he said, he'd exercise his shadow self by watching the wrestling on television. He had, he told Adrian, sought encouragement in writing his thesis by joining a Friday afternoon creative writing group, which was attended by ten or eleven fellow authors, which overall had proved to be an amiable and not unenlightening experience, and had provided him with the opportunity to get out and about and meet people with similar interests and aspirations.

Adrian decided that for the time being, rather than return to his books, he'd spend more time with his newly found acquaintance.

He'd just been staying in Bristol himself, he said. His first wife lived there. Not that he had gone there because of her, although he had met her again, the once, but there had been nothing more to it than that. He had, he told Dick, who sat there nodding, recently broken up with the woman he had lived with for years. It all went bottoms up by the end, he said. He'd had no way of knowing how these things would turn out, what he or for that matter she could have done to save the situation. She drank, he told Dick. Sadly. He thought perhaps she was bored. Hadn't enough on her hands, enough to engage her interests. When he first met her, she had been teaching English Literature part-time at a further education college, then later for some time she worked in administration for a textile company, but then they merged with some other outfit and she was offered, on good terms, redundancy, which offer she had accepted. In retrospect it was possible she'd have done better to remain with the company, as it would at least have given her some sort of structure in her life and everyone needed structure. As it was, apart from, for a while, a few days a week with a charity, she hadn't done anything, and that had given her too much time on her own, to lose touch with reality, to become self-absorbed. He was afraid to have to tell Dick that he had discovered, although she had never spoken to him or he to her about it, that she had taken some sort of lover, a chap who was several years younger than she, a situation one had heard that was not altogether uncommon, and he had come to suspect that that relationship, which had been to some extent a sustaining influence on her, had begun to fade, if in fact it hadn't petered out altogether, and Susie – her name was Susie, he told Dick – in attempting to regain her young man's affections had had a face lift, some awful disfiguring procedure, similar effects of which one had seen from time to time on various misguided celebrities, mostly to be found on light entertainment television programmes, and that, he suspected, her young man had declined to appreciate her efforts on his behalf, and that may well have been the reason behind her having to resort more and more to her habit of drinking large quantities of gin, a drink by the way which he himself had found unpleasant. Of course, he had never said a word to Susie about all that. Better, he said, to pretend ignorance of the facts. To have admitted his knowledge of her situation, would, in his view, have caused her further distress.

Throughout Adrian's narrative Dick remained silent, and while never taking his eyes off him, continued to nod. Adrian couldn't be sure what Dick thought of him. Which was reassuring. He liked the feeling that in talking to Dick he was talking to a stranger. He expressed the hope that on Dick's monthly visits to the capital, they could reconvene, and continue their conversations on the sixth floor of the library again. Dick said he thought that a nice idea, and looked forward to doing so. He had to go then, he said, to catch his 5.23. train to Bristol Temple Meads station, and on his way to Paddington station stop off at a greengrocer to purchase strawberries which he had noticed that morning on his way to the library were on an offer of three kilos for one pound ninety-nine. Would he be able to eat so many? Adrian asked. He wouldn't, Dick said, but one couldn't afford to turn one's back on a bargain.

*

Adrian and **Susie** were in Regent Street when from across the street he saw her standing outside Reiss clothing store. Seeing her there, he experienced a feeling he hadn't ever felt before, a sudden and unexpected uprising of joy and utter relief.

He called and waved and she turned and saw him. He hurried over, with barely a thought for the oncoming traffic. She stood there smiling at him, as if, it seemed to him, awestruck. She told him she had been seeing a Dr Reynolds and had found it impossible to speak. Dr Reynolds had said she might find it helpful if she spoke of herself in the third person singular. And she had been surprised to find it was easier to talk about someone else even when that someone else was, in fact, her. It felt safer, she wrote in her diary, into which Dr Reynolds had suggested she might enter her 'journey', if, he had said, she would kindly excuse the hackneyed terminology.

She had thrown four potted plants from the fourth floor flat she was renting, she said to Adrian as they sheltered from the rain in the doorway of the Calvin Klein building. Four pots, two large vases and a coffee table, she said. She had had enough. She was out of her mind.

She'd lost her way, she had said to Dr Reynolds. 'Ah', Dr Reynolds had said. He sat back in the leather chair by the side of his desk, she said to Adrian. She never saw Dr Reynolds' face as the room was dark with the Venetian blinds closed. It was his grey trousered legs and scuffed brown shoes, stretched out into the room which she mostly saw. He was there but not so much so, she said. She was sure should she ever see him away from his consulting room, outside in the street or anywhere, she'd not recognize him.

The police took her to St Ann's where she was put in a curtained cubicle in a ward, she said to Adrian. It was the most depressing place that she had ever known, she had said to Dr Reynolds. 'Ah,' Dr Reynolds had said to her. He was a shit, she had said; that man she was seeing on the sly while she was living with Adrian and Adrian not knowing, and she was seeing him after she and Adrian had separated. It was her birthday and he'd promised, promised, promised, he couldn't ever deny it, he'd meet her in Selfridges. She had seen a navy-blue coat and he had promised he'd buy it for her birthday and they'd go to lunch at the Strand Palace. She'd never been to the Strand Palace in the Strand, she had checked out where it was, she'd done a recce in advance to maintain her anticipation, her excitement at the thought of it, and on the day it was her birthday she had gone to Selfridges as agreed but he wasn't there, didn't arrive and the coat was too large and she phoned and she texted him and she phoned and texted and he didn't answer, there was no answer and they said at the office where he worked he was in Sweden, he and his wife had taken a vacation in Ysad Sweden, had gone with their two sons. They'd rented a villa in Ysad by the sea, they said. It was by the sea and he wasn't back, he was due to be back at the office in two weeks. Dr Reynolds wasn't saying anything. He wasn't saying anything, she had shouted at Dr Reynolds, him sitting back in the fucking gloom, Bob and his wife and family were in Ysad Sweden, she was on the platform at Baker Street and when she thought she heard the train coming she threw herself onto the rails but the train she was expecting didn't come not till she had been dragged by strangers, by strangers back onto the platform. It hadn't been the train she thought she could hear coming but one arriving at another platform and travelling in the opposite direction to that which the train she had been expecting was heading.

Adrian said he wondered whether Selfridges had by now got in a navy blue coat of her size. The rain had stopped, the sun was out. They could go and find out, he said, and, if she could bear to, they could go and have lunch at the Strand Palace, he said, which he'd not ever been to. Oh, she'd love it, Adrian, she said. It was so grand, and the waiters and the staff so polite and considerate and the lamb cutlets and the lemon tart for desert were delicious. She had been there by herself since she'd been seeing Dr Reynolds, which Dr Reynolds had said was a very good sign, and had congratulated her, and she thought that maybe she would like to go there again and not on her own but with Adrian. When she later told Dr Reynolds that they had gone and she had had the Scottish salmon and crème brulé and Adrian had had the chicken and apple tart with ice cream and they had shared half a bottle of red wine which was delicious, Dr Reynolds applauded, clapped his hands quietly. He never did anything and said anything loudly, that wasn't his style, he kept in the background where he belonged. And Dr Reynolds was pleased and she was pleased as she told Adrian in Zedel's Brasserie the day after they had had lunch at the Strand Palace and, as she was to say to Dr Reynolds, she and Adrian agreed to give it another go, to look out for a house this time, somewhere they could each spread their wings so as not to be all over each other, and they'd always eat together, that is they'd have dinner together when they were at home. And Dr Reynolds said she and he, that is Adrian, whom he had not met nor intended to, were to be congratulated and he thanked her for inviting him to their wedding which they had decided to go ahead with as previously they had just lived together, and, they having not been married, may possibly, only possibly, have been the cause or perhaps maybe one of the reasons for the deterioration in their relationship which speculation was viewed by both her and Adrian as encouraging. He loved a happy ending, Dr Reynolds said that last time she went to see him, and she told Adrian he had said that, that he had said he loved a happy ending which had been a lovely thing to say, she said to Adrian again over dinner in the Italian restaurant in Kentish Town as they discussed the viewings they had together been making that day of properties for sale some of which were horrid, a disgrace they agreed, overpriced, not at all suitable but that one, that nice late Victorian three bedroom house just north of Highgate seemed to be just the job. They could see themselves living there, and a nice garden too even though the house faced north east, and they had put in an initial offer, and at the Pizza Express the following day they raised a glass, a toast, and wished themselves luck and good fortune in the hope their offer on the house might be accepted and they would move in and buy new furniture and, of course, it was too late to have children but they could adopt, they could think about adopting, it was a possibility although they mustn't rush into making a decision, best to think about it, consider the pros and cons, the responsibilities and so on and so forth and wasn't it fun,

Adrian, just like when they first met, in the old days, him the good-looking brute that he was, she said, and she thin as a rake, elbows everywhere, and a smile he could have died for.

CHANGING PLACES

Bob, Ace McKenzie and Baggy Ted are at The Anchor off the High Street. They are seated separately on the well-upholstered high-backed stools at the tall round tables made for two. Each with his pint and another on its way. An empty glass is an empty life.

Half eleven and Baggy Ted is the first of them to arrive, to take his place, say his good mornings to the bar and waiting staff. Sweetly asks for his pint, 'The Foster's if you be so kind.' Unsightly, out of fashion. His large unruly head of black hair, his uneven features. A cumbersome belly all at odds with itself, all one way and then the other, beneath a loose un-ironed, once-upon-a-time white shirt. Baggy Ted worked for the Council – refuse collector.

Bob turns up ten minutes after the stroke of twelve. He is firmly put together, wearing a grey jumper close-fitting over his midriff and down-to-earth trousers. He seats himself on a stool and at a table identical to that at which Baggy Ted is seated, and at a distance of some two metres or thereabouts. Bob is in his fifties. He had sometime earlier been made redundant, his job as a warehouse manager for Dolliters Foods no longer existing. The waitress brings over his Guinness. He, Baggy Ted and Ace McKenzie are regulars. The staff know what they drink. It saves them coming to the bar.

Ace McKenzie is known simply as Ace. Unlike Baggy Ted and Bob, he follows a less predetermined schedule.

'He is irregular in his habits,' Bob has said to Baggy Ted.

'He's irregular in his habits,' Baggy Ted says of Ace to the waitress on her way to a table set back in an alcove with the All-Day Chicken Tikka Masala.

Ace is six feet two, of a loping unhurried gait. Late forties, fifties. Not a thing one can be sure of.

'Got a little bit of a job on,' he says.

'Right-ho,' Bob says.

'There's this bloke,' Ace says.

'Right-ho,' says Baggy Ted.

Ace, on his matching stool within speaking-up distance from Bob and Baggy Ted, is brought his two pints of Younger's Best. The first goes down in one. He sits back and surveys the second pint, with its regulation head of 0.5 inches.

'Thirsty work,' he says.

Bob nods.

Baggy Ted's belly shifts sideways.

You'd think nothing ever happened, not anything of note.

And thank God for that, thinks Baggy Ted.

Ace comes in, says he's got a bit of a job on. The way he says it, he makes it sound as if it isn't entirely legit, a nice little number on the side. Only, he hasn't got a nice little number on the side. He says he has, like he does from time to time, but he hasn't.

He lives in a room in Haringey, off Green Lanes. One room, kitchenette with a cooker and a fridge, washing machine and dryer. Nice enough room, well-decorated. Radiators, hot water, ensuite shower. He works nights. Security. Warehouse. 6. pm till 1.a.m. Mondays – Thursdays. Scrapes by, he says. He's got a sister in Sydenham, and an uncle and aunts and cousins in Jamaica.

He's got a girlfriend, off and on, Beatrice who works for Care for the Elderly in Palmers Green. Beatrice has a kid by a fella who didn't stick around to make the kid's acquaintance. Ace likes the kid. But Ace is restless. Always restless, that's what Beatrice says of him, and she's right. Ace knows she's right. She knows she's right about Ace, but he's ok, he'll do. When he's there he's ok, nice with the kid, Josh. Him and Josh get on. Play football in Fairland Park. He serves, she says of him. How's that man of yours? He serves, she says. She's got a body on her, she knows that, she knows that Ace knows that. He's a big man, she's a big woman, she says. Says to her friend Audrey, who herself is thin. She'd be too thin for Ace. Ace likes big, Beatrice says. And she laughs. She's got a big laugh; she throws back her head, laughs at Ace, 'the dope', and Ace likes that laugh. They laugh, laugh together, when he visits, when they are in the bed, the king size bed that takes up all of that small front bedroom where she lives. Let's go, she says to him. And Ace serves.

*

Ace and Beatrice are getting married.

'I'm getting married,' Ace says to Bob and Baggy Ted, says to the waitress who's on her way with the Friday fish and chips for customers on a table in an alcove by the kitchens.

'He's getting married,' Baggy Ted says to Bob.

Not that Bob hadn't heard Ace say he was getting married, but Baggy Ted isn't sure he's rightly heard him say he's getting married. Not that he's not trusting his hearing, his hearing not being in too bad a condition all in all, but Ace's announcement is difficult to take in, to accommodate.

'Getting married, are you?' Bob says.

*

'We're getting married, Beatrice says to Audrey.
'Ace?'
'I say the boy needs a father,' she says to Audrey. 'I say to Ace, that boy needs a father, Ace. You come round here, make yourself free with my steak and kidney pie, my apple dumplings, you got to do what's proper. The boy loves you, Ace,' I say.

*

'I'm going to be a dad,' Ace says to Bob and Baggy Ted.
'You are?' Baggy Ted says.
'Congratulations,' Bob says.
'When's the baby due?' the waitress says.
'It's not due,' Ace says. 'The baby's not due. He's not a baby. He's a boy. Josh. We play footer in Fairland Park. He needs a dad.'
'You'll make a great dad, Ace,' the waitress says.
'So, she's not expecting or anything?' Baggy Ted says.
'No, she's not expecting,' Bob proudly says to Baggy Ted, to the waitress on her way to the tables in the alcoves. 'He's taking the place, so to speak, of the boy's dad who isn't around, is that so, Ace?'
'That's it,' Ace says.
'Where's the wedding?' Baggy Ted says.
'Register office, George Meehan House,' Ace says. 'Friday week. Half twelve.'
'Not in a church then?' Bob says.

'Not in a church,' Ace says.

'He's not having his wedding in a church,' Baggy Ted says to the waitress on her way back from a table under the stairs at the back.

'Register office,' Ace says. 'Reception, the Oxford Arms, Kentish Town. The both of you, my witnesses.'

*

'He's bringing two of his buddies from The Anchor as his witnesses,' Beatrice says to Audrey in Beatrice's kitchen. 'I never met them, only he says he can't very well not invite them, cos him and them hang out from time to time, he says, at The Anchor. They're old mates, he says. I tell him they better come looking nice, better have a good wash, put on a suit and tie. I don't want no down-and-outs at the reception. I got people coming, nice, well-turned-out people, my sister Rose, my uncle Webster, my cousin, he's coming over all the way from Cologne, Germany,' she says to Audrey. 'Ace says as how his two mates, Ted and Bob don't have no suits, not that he knows of. He can't be expected to ask them to come all dressed up, he says, them not having anything special to dress up in, he says. They're not going out and buying a suit special, he can't ask them that. I say just as long as they tidy up in what they have got, put on the best they can, I say to him. He comes over, says to me he's had a word with them, with his two mates Bob and Ted, he says the one of them says he's got a tie what he bought for a funeral and a white shirt, and the other says as he'll comb his hair. You've got to laugh I say to him. You're going to wear a suit, that's a definite, I say. Him and Josh play footer in Fairland Park. Ace turn up in his new suit, dark blue, all swanky, he and Josh play footer, Josh cuts his knees, falls over, cuts his knees, Ace gets blood on his suit. I tell him what you playing footer for in your suit, Ace? You going to look good at my wedding, or aren't you?'

*

Ace lopes in, sits himself at his table, hoists himself up on the upholstered high back stool.

'Great wedding,' Baggy Ted says. 'Best wedding I've been to,' he says.

'Your Beatrice's sister Rose,' Bob says. 'A very nice friendly lady, if I may say so, Ace.'

'I reckon Bob and her are all set for each other, eh, Ace?' Baggy Ted says.

'Nothing's been said,' Bob says.

'Nothing been said,' Baggy Ted says. Says it in a knowing sort of way, as if to say no need for anything to be said, cos from what he saw and heard at the wedding he reckons Bob and Rose are all set for each other, the way they talk and hang out there at the reception, her laughing, Bob all proud, sticking out his chest all in align with his belly, what didn't look so prominent when he was sticking out his chest. And she don't seem to mind the look of him no how, not Rose, she laughing the way she was, and him all proud and taken up with her.

Before the year is out it'll be Bob and Rose going down the aisle, that's what Baggy Ted thinks. Only it won't be the aisle as such, it'll be the register office like with Ace and his Beatrice.

With Bob getting married to Rose, with Ace married as he is to Beatrice, they'll not be coming into The Anchor as they have been, Baggy Ted thinks. Which thought isn't frankly much to his liking, cos the place won't be the same, not without Bob and Ace.

The place was all likely to go downhill. Downhill fast. Them tall tables, them upholstered stools they sit on, what's going to become of them, he thinks, who's going to park their backsides on them, he wonders. Not a welcome thought. Not a thought he's too happy to consider. Not too happy, not at all about the prospect.

*

'What you think of Bob then?' Beatrice says to Rose, there in Beatrice's kitchen with Audrey and the instant Nescafe.

'Rose likes him well enough,' Audrey says, 'She could do worse than him, I reckon,' she says.

'He's nicely mannered,' Beatrice says.

'He's already been married,' Rose says. 'He's divorced. She went off with another fella fifteen years back. I said to him, oh, sorry to hear that, Bob. Why though? Why she go off with this other bloke? I say to him. What she gone off for? He says, she met this other bloke on the internet. Yeah, well, be that as it may. I say what was wrong with you, Bob, that she go off, eh? You seem ok to me, Bob, I say, you seem a nice enough fella. You ain't too good looking, I'll grant, but there's a lot worse. Well, he says, she said she wanted adventure, wanted some of the luxuries of life. The fella she goes off with, he'd got a Mercedes. So, what do you feel about that? I say to him. What did he feel when she walked out with this guy? Well, he says, what can one do? You love her? I say. Yeah, well, I did. If she wants to go off, well, I can't do anything about it. I can't come up with what she wants, he says.'

'There's something about him though,' Audrey says.

'Yeah, well, I know that,' Rose says.

'Where's he live?' Audrey says.

'Back of the petrol station. Got a flat. He moved there after his wife left him. I've not seen it. He says it's nice, double glazed, he says. Constant hot water.'

'You feel comfortable with the man,' Beatrice says. 'You at your time of life, forgive me, Rose, that's a blessing in itself, Rose. Time come when them other things, the Mercedes, you know what I mean, they don't have so much say in the matter, yeah? Time come, like me and Ace, when you go for what is the less hassle. Your Bob fella, he's a domesticated type of man I would say from what I have seen, you best take that on board, Rose.'

'It's how you're feeling inside, Rose,' Audrey says. 'In here,' she says, her hand over her heart.

*

'You seeing Rose again this weekend?' Baggy Ted says to Bob.
'She's busy this weekend,' Bob says.
Ace up at his table knows it hasn't worked out like it was hoped. Rose said she had to see her cousins in Plumstead. Only Ace knows she hasn't got cousins in Plumstead. That was just her way of easing out. It was over.

It'd have been good if it had worked out somehow, that's the way Bob feels. He would have liked it to go on, progress sort of thing, like they say, but it hasn't. And Ace isn't saying anything, but he knows. He knows it wouldn't be any use him saying anything. What's done is done.

Bob will survive. That's what Beatrice says, not in an offhand unfriendly way, but sympathetically, the two of them, her and Ace in her big king-size, him saying it's a pity about Bob. It's unfortunate, Bob being a nice sort of guy but that's life. Some you win, some you lose. Bob has lost. But she has said he'll survive. And Ace thinks, yeah, she's right, Bob's a survivor, and optimist, likeable. One of the best. He's one of the best, he says to Beatrice.

*

Ace doesn't come in The Anchor, not every day like he used to. Not now he's married. He comes in on a Friday and on a Monday or sometimes a Tuesday. Bob's still coming in. Better than it might have turned out, Baggy Ted reckons. One has to adapt to circumstances. Could have been worse, he says to himself,

*

'It's pity about Bob, but we got to get you settled, Rose, that's for sure,' Beatrice says to Rose, the two of them in Beatrice's kitchen.

'I'm alright as I am,' Rose says.

'Audrey's settled,' Beatrice says.

'And a lot of good it's done her,' Rose says. 'Her married to her Carl.'

Her Carl is not anyone Audrey speaks about. He's out every day, electrician, and at weekends he's with his kids by his first wife or with his mate Johnny at the fishing. He's sold on fishing is Carl, Audrey has said of him and that's about it, nothing more to be said about him. Fishing, she said, when Beatrice or Rose asks after him.

'Audrey's Carl is dull, no arguing with that,' Beatrice says to Rose. 'Audrey reckoned she was going to marry someone with a bit of up and go, and what she do? She walks into her marriage with Carl. She can't explain it. There she was, twenty-two-years old, working in the shoe shop. Carl is a neighbour, lives about four streets away. She sees him, and he assumes they're engaged, assumes they're getting married. And, somehow, that's it. She doesn't put up any sort of resistance,' Beatrice says. 'Can't make her mind up. Doesn't know what she wants, what to do in life. Carl says they're getting married, so they do.'

'Audrey might as well be on her own. I wonder she hasn't gone off with some other bloke,' Rose says.

'Not got it in her,' Beatrice says.

'I reckon her and Bob would be good for each other,' Rose says. 'Bob's nice. He's not the man for me. But he'd be all right for Audrey.'

*

'You want to bring your mate Bob round?' Beatrice says to Ace in their king-size. 'I want him to meet Audrey.'

'Give over,' Ace says. 'What you running here, a dating agency? Marriage Bureau'?

*

'You want to come over Friday evening, Bob?' Ace says in The Anchor. 'Come over Friday. Beatrice is going to cook up something. Good cook, she is. Take my word. Friday,' Ace says.

'Well, that's very nice, very civil of you, Ace.'

'Not taking no for an answer,' Ace says.

'Right,' Bob says.

'Friday,' Ace says. 'Me, you, Beatrice. And Beatrice's friend Audrey.'

*

'Bob's going out with this Audrey person,' Baggy Ted says to the waitress. He can't help himself. Thinks he ought not to say it to the waitress. Nothing to do with the waitress. But he says it, cos he has to. Audrey's husband has gone back to his first wife, so now it's Audrey and Bob. Baggy Ted thinks here we go again. Why can't things be left as they are. All this chopping and changing.

*

'I remember when this place here was the best,' Baggy Ted says, thinking back to when he and Bob and Ace used to come here mostly every day, Bob on the dot of half eleven, Ace sometime later in the morning. Them on their high stools, Baggy Ted with his Fosters, Bob with his Guinness, Ace with the Youngers. The conversation they had them days.

'It's not what it used to be,' he says to the waitress passing by to table 14 with Thursday's Special Indian Curry.

*

Benny is sitting where Bob used to sit, and Clive is where Ace used to be. Benny's a retired postman. Baggy Ted found that out after Benny had been coming in for a couple of weeks. He comes in most days, for just over the hour and a half, mid-mornings. His wife died April last year. He lives above where Cote Brasserie is now. He's lived in these parts for fifty-six years, he and his wife in the flat above Cote Brasserie. Worked in the post office across the road from them, when it was a sorting office, before it changed to an ordinary post office, with the queue outside lining up down the street on its way to Boots the Opticians.

A nicer man you could not hope to meet than Benny. A gentleman. A bit softly speaking for Baggy Ted, had to ask him if he'd be good enough to speak up a little on account of Baggy Ted's hearing, which, truth to tell, was up to standard considering his age, but he doesn't want to cause offence to Benny so he makes out he's a bit hard of the hearing rather than him telling Benny he's speaking too quietly, and Benny, being the gent he is, speaks up most of the time, enough to keep the wheels turning.

Clive, on the stool where Ace used to sit, is gay. Well, one could tell that. The way he conducts himself, the manner of him, the way he holds his head, his overall facial expression. Baggy Ted recognizes this, he thinks Clive is what one might call the old type of gay, like you used to see them on TV, on the Variety shows. A gentleman. Pleasant. Slightly tart. Given to pursing his lips. Drinks Stella Artois. Used to work for Cunard, a ship's purser. Steward on the cruise ships. Never got used to having his two feet on the ground, he says to Baggy Ted and Benny. His legs, he says, all over the place. He's not going to get himself a walking stick. God, no, that isn't him, not at all, he says, pursing his lips. He'd had a partner, but his partner died of the 'unspeakables', he says. He's not afraid of Baggy Ted and Benny knowing.

With Ace and Bob coming into The Anchor now and then, and with Benny and Clive sitting at Ace and Bob's tables, Baggy Ted reckons, when push comes to shove, five's a crowd. With the five of them the sense of camaraderie is sort of missing. 'Disparate' is the word that comes to his mind.

What's more, Bob and Ace can't ever be sure of finding a table anywhere near them. To Baggy Ted's way of thinking, it's nigh on impossible to have any sort of conversation with Bob and Ace, when the two of them are sitting way over by the entrance door.

On the other hand, when all's said and done, when it comes down to it, it's all right here in The Anchor, Baggy Ted thinks. Benny and Clive are most amiable, if that's the word.

'You alright?' the waitress asks as she hands him his Fosters.

'Everything fine and dandy,' Baggy Ted says. 'You got to go with the flow, as the expression has it,' he says. 'Got to move with the times.'

When one half closes one's eyes, it could be said that Benny and Clive, seated separately on the well-upholstered high-backed stools, are Bob and Ace as it used to be, Baggy Ted says to himself.

THE BAR ON THE THIRD FLOOR

They were sitting at the centre table in the third-floor cocktail bar at Fortnum and Mason in Regent Street, waiting for a fall guy, a sitting duck; Terry in his grey and maroon striped blazer and grey flannels, Evelyn in a long dark green dress. This was in 2019, just before the outbreak of Covid 19 in the UK. Terry had received his State Pension that year and both he and Evelyn had their Travel Freedom Passes.

They each had a drink and waited.

An elderly couple came in and sat in the brown leather armchairs beneath the white shuttered window blinds at the far wall.

Terry – known as 'Terence' to his 'business clients' – rose and went over to the alcove and fiddled with the magazines. He returned to his and Evelyn's table. Every now and then he and Evelyn looked over at the couple and smiled, and did so discreetly. It was to Terry like fly fishing. Nothing should be done to alarm or engender suspicion.

Terry thought he'd caught the eye of the elderly gent, and smiled. The gent looked away. 'I'm in Investments,' Terry wanted to say. 'I'm Terence, this is Evelyn. We've a boat in the Canaries. We rent it out from time to time. Thank goodness for Portalidity

Investment Funds. Terrific interest rates,' he would tell the couple. Then he'd change the subject, speak of this and that, get them talking about themselves. Camaraderie was the thing.

They came to the Fortnum and Mason's bar, very smart, exclusive, brown leather, expensive cocktails, Tuesdays and Thursdays, Terry believing or rather hoping they'd be the best days. He couldn't explain to Evelyn or to himself why he might believe that, but two days of the week was all that they could manage, or, put another way, all they thought they could get away with.

Should it come about that 'the fish' declined to bite that afternoon, they would set out for an early dinner at Plimptons in Covent Garden. They would try Plimptons Restaurant because it had opened its doors for the first time just a week or two earlier and as yet they themselves hadn't been there. They'd go to Zedel's, they liked it there; all that Art Deco glamour, the chandeliers, the mirrors, the musicians playing. They'd go to Zedel's in a shot, only they'd already been to Zedel's, had had dinner there among all the bustle and noise. They'd had the Lamb Tagine, and sent it back. They had eaten some, a good amount, delicious, stopped half way through, called over the waitress 'Sorry, not cooked, can't eat it.' The second one, the replacement had been the same. Terence had said, 'This isn't up to the standard we've come to expect from Zedel's.' It wouldn't do, he'd said. No, they were not prepared to speak with the manager. And up Terence had got and then Evelyn, and out they had marched looking disappointed and dignified and, with the restaurant fully booked and buzzing, no one, as expected, had asked them to pay the bill. They'd go there again, had in fact tried, but were told that all the tables had already been reserved. It was the pesty cameras that upset things for Terry and Evelyn. Instant recognition and all that. They had had the same bad luck at Trattoria Mortana. At a Steak House at the back of Leicester Square, the man on the door had refused them entry, making it clear that their reputation had preceded them.

Things were getting tight, Terry had said to Evelyn. The world, as they had come to know it, was shrinking.

When things had been quiet awhile back, they'd up sticks and gone to Margate, where Terry had a sister, Phyllis, but Phyllis said she had a lodger so they couldn't stay. Not that Terry and Evelyn believed her. To them, Phyllis was a washout. She took after her and Terry's Aunt Mary who was 'as-mean-as-could-be' to both him and Phyllis when they were kids, when they had to stay in her drably furnished flat in Eastbourne. Their father at the time had been serving a three year stretch in Pentonville prison on account of a small matter of tax evasion. And their mother, according to their Aunt Mary, had gone off to Cairo with the owner of an off-licence in Ladbroke Grove.

To Terry's way of thinking, Evelyn was essential to their operations. People took to her. Thought her trustworthy, unaffected.

The two of them had met in Gravesend after Terry had come out from doing twelve months 'inside' on account of a 'financial miscalculation' at the golf club where he'd been working as bar manager back in 2002. Evelyn was in Gravesend living with her elderly parents and worked in a tea shop near the river. He had asked her out, and, in no time at all, they had got married at the registry office in Windmill Street.

Thereafter, Evelyn had left her parents in the care of her sister. She and Terry made it back to Willesden where he'd been renting a one-bedroom flat from Ben Tarkner, who at that time had been in prison in Nottingham. Terry couldn't think what it could have been that caused Ben to land up there. But Ben Tarkner in those days was in and out of the slammer like it was his second home, he had told Evelyn.

After Willesden they rented in Harlesden. And since October 2018 they'd taken a place in West Hampstead. Things, Terry had said, were 'picking up'. For Terry, things were always 'picking up'. To suggest otherwise was deemed inadmissible. He followed a means of livelihood that suited him and the possibility of an alternative life style was not something he thought to consider. Hypothetically, should he have been required to justify his 'modus vivendi', as he liked to refer to it, he would have maintained that it was his intangible right to live the life that best befitted him.

It was that life, Terry's chosen and self-appointed career, that Evelyn revered. And in like manner, she held close to herself her feelings of fondness and respect for the way he presented himself to the world, his smart jacket and tie, clean finger nails, his carefully groomed grey hair and immaculately polished shoes.

'One has to look after oneself, Evelyn,' he had said. One had to look the part.

There had been those days of childhood innocence, those 'halcyon days', as Terry spoke of them; playing footer in Princes Park in Eastbourne, the pier at Hastings, the penny slot machines. The girl with the legs at the tennis club, the back row at the Ritz in Seaford. The minor public boarding school. Terry in the school's first eleven cricket team.

He'd taken a job with a shipping company in Bristol, but had found it unenterprising. He'd worked for a time for a travel firm, contrived to award himself free rides here and there; in Slovakia,

Luxemburg, Malta and such like. Then the chap who had owned the firm sold it, and the new chap, as Terry had discovered, had had his own ideas.

Evelyn herself, whatever the circumstances and the setbacks their transactions encountered, remained steadfast and resolute.

'I'm a survivor,' she said to Terry in the early days, said it to him again, and said it more than once or twice in more recent times. 'I'm a survivor,' she'd say when things got sticky.

She'd worked in Woolworths, well, that was a long time ago, when Woolworths was Woolworths, she'd say. And then she'd helped out in a care home, which, 'Terry dear,' she said, 'was rather too depressing.' Then it had been the tea room, Gravesend.

'And after that, Terry, dear, it was you,' she'd say. 'And a never-ending life of adventure,' she'd tell him.

The time Terry and Evelyn most loved to recall was when they had been delivering upmarket automobiles across Eastern Europe, about which one didn't ask too many questions. One night they were driving in the Carpathian Mountains, they came across a farm house. The farmer invited them in, then the local police turned up and demanded to see their papers. Evelyn told them they were on their honeymoon, had them raise a glass of the farmer's home-made brandy that tasted of creosote in celebration of the event, and everyone including the farmer got zonked. Then the two police officers took a trial drive of the BMW Coupe and nearly crashed it.

'We're Bonnie and Clyde,' Evelyn said, as they drove to their drop off point over the Romanian border.

It'd been Italy that put an end to that particular episode. Certain individuals got in on the act and things got heavy. Terry and Evelyn took off for the Costa Brava. Lost a lot of money, were pretty well cleaned out.

When later they shared the memory of that time with some of their prospective 'clients', a number of them, strangely and unaccountably, were impressed by their escapades and more ready to invest in their business proposals than they had been earlier.

'Don't look for the rational in folk,' Terry would say to Evelyn as they would sit back comfortably in The American Bar at The Savoy, the SkyLounge at the Hilton, Good Godfrey's at the Waldorf, The Grand in Brighton, Evelyn with her tangy, not-too-sweet Mexican Martini, Terry with an extra-large whisky sour.

'People believe what they need to believe,' he'd say. 'And in doing so, they fabricate and secure for themselves those identities to which they aspire. It's greed and the need for social status to which people are mostly addicted,' he would conclude.

And Evelyn would giggle at his exaggerated self-assurance and urbanity.

Over time, when the occasional small-scale opportunities arose, Terry advised on investment schemes, traded in boat sales, mediated in the purchase and sale of overseas properties, of villas and hotels in terminal decline. Together with Evelyn, he made deals. Came to understandings. Knew his stuff. Had form.

Of course, it took time to nurture a client, to build mutual trust and confidence, or, as Terry said, 'the interpersonal relationships' that might lead to a done deal. It was on the same principle as someone wishing to purchase a very expensive piece of jewellery at somewhere like Tiffany's or De Beers in Old Bond Street. One didn't expect the customer to come in and purchase on the spot, not at all. Some did, of course. But there were those who would come in and have a look at a top-quality diamond necklace, or a gold ring or whatever, and go away; and later, on another day, sometimes after two or three weeks, come back for a further look, and feeling comforted by the lack of pressure, by the civilized and exclusive welcome, it was possible that after some time-lapse, she, for invariably it was a she, would return with her husband, and that was when the purchase would most likely be made. That was Terry's theory and one which, when he had the time, he applied to his own mode of business.

On that afternoon in the third-floor bar at Fortnum and Mason, however, Terry and Evelyn were cognizant of the unwelcome reality that that day's 'fishing expedition' and their twice-weekly visits to the bar were not likely at any time to produce the desired results. Furthermore, they only had enough dosh for one more dry Martini between them; and they hadn't enough of 'the ready' with which to pay the West Hampstead rent.

'Phone Crocker for a loan,' Evelyn said from behind her empty cocktail glass.

Crocker would have helped out had he'd been there. He was an old friend of Terry's deceased father.

'Crocker's in Rio,' Terry said.

The elderly couple rose. On passing Terry and Evelyn's table, Terry attempted to engage them in conversation. 'I hear there's some sort of protest in Trafalgar Square,' he said. 'Do you happen to know anything about it?'

The elderly couple passed by without a word, with only the merest glance of acknowledgement from the gent before they departed, leaving Terry and Evelyn stranded, or as Terry would say, 'In the 'proverbial' shit, Evelyn, darling.' No chance then of introducing the couple to the 'frankly, sir, once in a lifetime' high returns investments on offer from Portalidity Investment Funds.

'Can I get you anything else?' the barman at their table said.

'No, thank you. We'll shortly be on our way. Lots to do,' Terry said.

'We love it here,' Evelyn said. 'Don't we, Terence?'

'The toilet,' Terry said to Evelyn after the barman had gone, and she rose and went out of the bar to the ladies.

'Gosh, need to go to the gents,' Terry said to the barman. 'The old prostate, I rather think. I expect this carrier bag of mine will be safe in here for the moment, won't it?' he said.

And, leaving on his chair a recently acquired Harrods bag that contained nothing but crunched up newspaper, he made a dignified and unhurried exit.

In the Spring of 2020, soon after lockdown, the cocktail bar on the third floor at Fortnum and Mason was obliged to close.

Terry and Evelyn went to live with Terry's sister Phyllis in Margate and 'lived on the scraps', until, he said, life got back to normal, when they could look forward to things 'picking up' once more.

The following year, on the Tuesdays and Thursdays of the first two weeks of October, they could be found seated at a table in the Coburg Bar at The Connaught Hotel in Mayfair, sizing up the clientele.

CYRIL, EYES FULL OF DRINK

Cyril, eyes full of drink. Him with a cane, for all to behold. It'll not hold him when he trips at the pavement's edge on exiting the French House pub in Soho, on making his way to God knows where, the Coach and Horses, there with a few old pals. There to imbibe, to put away a few jars, to indulge in brittle banter, short and succinct.

Old Michael Cobbler, up at the bar – for who sits at a table? – to sit is to surrender – to show a lack of aptitude for the task in hand, the treble scotch, the London Pride. Michael, loud and jolly, loud violent Mike once he's passed his seventh pint, his eighth scotch, and 'For God's sake,' he cries, 'forget the fucking glass, give us the bottle,' tips back the fucking bottle, tips up a table. Michael C tipped up and tossed out onto the pavement, barred. Never to set foot inside again. Until the next time.

Old Cyril, himself, full of himself, outshone in his cups by Michael C, the damn good fellow and let no one say any different. Let anyone who says different, say it to Cyril's face. Look at him now, Cyril with his cane, his perseverance, wondering where the next penny, for the next fucking drink, is coming from.

He was in The Mousetrap, wasn't he? He'd drunk with Peter O'Toole. Drank with the best of them, stars of stage and screen, with Robert Stephens in the Queens. Worked with Ronnie Fraser. There was a man, a real actor if ever there was, worked with him in whatever-it-was. Can't for the moment put a finger on it, the television series, what was it? He'd worked with Ronnie, a gentleman who could hold his liquor. Those were the days. God, sometimes he wonders, where's it all gone? He's been in The Mousetrap; did he tell you? West End. Ambassadors, before it moved to the St Martins. The Mousetrap same age, more or less, as himself. Well, more or less. What's a few years between friends? That's what he tells people, people not in the business, people who don't know. And here he is on his way to his fucking room-and-a-half; 'the apartment', don't you know? In Kensal Rise. Fucking Kensal Rise. Posters on the wall, the mementoes, photos, books on Gielgud, Robert Donat, the great actor manager Donald Wolfit. Cyril now alighting at Kensal Green Tube Station, on his uncertain way, the left leg giving him the pip, God help him, to his room-and-a-half in Rochester Avenue.

On the morrow – oh, don't start that – tomorrow, it's the tourists, the guided walk, the Americans, God bless them. The greatest nation in the world. They love him. A privilege, they say. Wonderful voice, could hear every word, even with all the traffic. Forty-five years in the theatre, sir. Played all the great theatres, Coriolanus, the King in The Scottish play, Tamburlaine The Great – my God, one can see him in that, the roar, the mayhem. Tell them what they want to hear. A handful of inaccuracies never went awry. Thank you so very much, Mr Cyril, it has been a privilege. If you ever visit Texas, if you ever visit Louisiana, Seattle, wherever -. Thank you, thank you, a most interesting walking tour. God bless America.

Outside the Villiers Street entrance to Embankment Underground Station, 2 p.m., Cyril Davenport, tall in his light-grey Gannex raincoat, beneath which the brown suit, shirt and collar, the brown tie. Him with his full head of swept-back silver-grey hair. Roll up, roll up, this afternoon's scheduled walk 'Murder in London's West End'; a slight drizzle in the air, God help him. Roll up, roll up, bang the fucking drum. Where the hell are they? Cyril Davenport, ladies and gentlemen, actor, performed in The Mousetrap, knew Peter O'Toole, Lawrence of Arabia, no less. Thank you, thank you, this way. 'Murder in London's West End.'

Here they are, first to arrive, an elderly couple and the wife's sister by the looks of her. Midlands by the sound of them. God help us, how's he going to pay his way at the French, at the Coach and Horses, just the three of them. Where are the Americans? We need the Americans. No Americans, no Coach and Horses, no fucking rent.

Here's a fella. In his sixties, not the life and soul, not by the looks of him, in a drab beige raincoat and hat to match and carrying a fold-up canvas stool.

'David Partiker,' the man says, not that Cyril has asked him.

Here they are, here they are, thank God for that, the Americans have arrived. Three of them, middle aged. A man and two women. You can tell the Americans from half a mile away.

'Welcome, ladies and gentlemen. God bless America'.

Very theatrical, they love the theatrical. A real actor, he had heard someone say of him during the guided walk he did the day before yesterday.

'The guided walk today, ladies and gentlemen, is 'Murder in London's West End of London.''

Two more arriving, two young English women. Three Japanese girls now. 'Ah, lovely ladies.' He'd say 'Lovely ladies from the Orient', but he'd got into trouble the last time, complaints to the office. 'Orient' not acceptable when addressing or referring to the

Japanese, the term generally considered to be offensive, he was told. God help us, you can't say or do fuck-all these days. Here's a woman on her own, in her fifties. Polish, she says. From Warsaw, she says. A wonderful country, such history, he tells her. Just in time. Another minute and we wouldn't be here.

'Cyril Davenport, your guide this afternoon,' he announces. 'We have here among us, our good friends from America, from Austin, Texas, no less; the gracious young people over here but for a brief sojourn from Japan, Tokyo, no less; young ladies from' –

'Hastings' the two young women call out and laugh.

'From the historical Kentish resort of Hastings; and our friends from the Midlands—'

'Brierly Hill.'

'Splendid,' Cyril says.

'I'm from Harrow.' This from the chap who said his name was David Partiker.

'You may, if you wish, address me by my first name – Cyril. Taken from the Greek with the meaning 'Lordly'. Cyril, for those of you interested in these matters, was the 9th-century missionary Saint Cyril, who devised the Cyrillic alphabet used in Slavonic languages.'

'Are you by any chance related?' the older American woman asks.

'Ah, dear lady, one might say that it could be imagined that is not altogether an impossibility. Thank you,' Cyril says.

'Thank you all for joining me on this somewhat overcast afternoon. We shall commence by making our way through Victoria Embankment Gardens, opened one hundred and fifty years ago, with our first stop at the rear of the Savoy Hotel. Off we go. There's a great deal to cover. Do try to keep up.'

With that, off he strides, the customers outpaced, and hurrying after him.

'Here we have the rear of the Savoy Hotel,' he grandly calls to his breathless audience. 'This internationally famous hotel opened on the 6th of August 1889. It was built by the impresario Richard D'Oyly Carte with the profits from his Gilbert and Sullivan opera productions. It was the first luxury hotel in Britain to introduce electric lights throughout the building. The celebrated guests staying here have included Mr George Gershwin, Mr Oscar Wilde, Charlie Chaplin, Judy Garland, and, ladies and gentlemen, the great British actor Laurence Olivier, whom I once had the privilege to meet some years ago.' He is hoping for a round of applause; it is unforthcoming. 'But more of that later perhaps. And, of course, ladies and gentlemen, one might say, foremost among such distinguished guests at the Savoy Hotel has been none other than the greatest Prime Minister our Country has ever known, who led us to victory in the second world war, Sir Winston Churchill.'

'Did you meet him?' asks the older American woman.

'Only briefly,' he graciously informs her, and moves swiftly on so as to avoid further enquiry as to the nature of his impostrous meeting with the great man of history.

'It was here at the Savoy Hotel in 1923, that thirty-two-year-old Princess Marie Marguerite Fahmy, a Frenchwoman of questionable morals, shot dead her twenty-two-year-old husband Prince Ali Fahmy of Egypt,' he declaims, raising his voice, giving it a bit of belly as they say, increasing the dramatic tension. God, why wasn't he on stage at the Old Vic at that moment, giving his Coriolanus?

'Have you ever played Bottom?' one of the young women from Hastings asks – cheeky sod.

'No,' he says. 'To proceed with the drama, it was during a violent thunderstorm on that night in July 1923 that there was heard coming from their suite of rooms the sound of three pistol shots fired in rapid succession. A hotel porter, who rushed to investigate, found Ali slumped against a wall in a pool of blood, a bullet through his head, and a hysterical Marguerite bending over his body and crying out, 'J'ai lui tiré' – 'I've shot him.' An open-and-shut case! You might think that. But no. No. No.'

God, he could do with a drink.

'The lady in court was defended by the brilliant Sir Edward Marshal Hall, convincing judge and jury that her husband, the murdered man had himself so mistreated her, had attempted to force himself on her with the intention of committing unspeakable sexual acts upon her – acts which, given the possible delicate feelings of our present company, I shall not more specifically particulate – I leave it to your imagination – needless to say the Prince was known to be bisexual – I'll say no more. The woman was acquitted. Was said, in passing, at one time, to have had a relationship of some sort with the Prince of Wales who, on becoming king, promptly abdicated, although, you may be assured, not as a consequence of any implied sexual relationship with the afore-mentioned woman, Princess Marie Marguerite Fahmy. Right now, off we go. Next stop. Please keep up.'

'Hurry along,' he calls as he heads up Cartland Lane, makes the long haul towards The Strand, crossing at the traffic lights to its northern side. He is ignoring the fucking pain in his left leg.

'We are now at the Vaudeville and Adelphi Theatres, ladies and gentlemen,' he calls.

The elderly couple and the wife's sister from the Midlands

remain on the opposite side of The Strand. They are waiting for the lights to change. My God. He can't wait. There's no help for it if they won't keep up.

'Please, if you will, direct your attention, ladies and gentlemen to the plaque here on the wall of the Adelphi Theatre. As you see, it marks the scene of the murder in 1897 of William Terriss, a contemporary of the great Sir Henry Irving, by the penniless drunken actor Richard Archer Prince, who, in a nutshell, was jealous of William Terriss' success. On the night of 1897, outside the stage door here, Richard Archer Prince stabbed William Terriss to death. It is said, William Terriss' ghost haunts the theatre before which, at this time, you now stand. Thank you. Right. Off we go.'

The Midlands folk have caught up and joined him.

'Can you go a little slower, not so fast?' the wife asks.

'Alack, we have a great deal to cover,' Cyril replies.

'Denmark Street, ladies and gentlemen—'

God, where are they? Here they are, the Japs. And the Hastings girls – can't think why they've come on the fucking walk, haven't shown one iota of interest, the two of them behaving throughout like giggling fifth formers. Here are the Americans. The Polish woman. David Partiker, the man in the raincoat, hat and fold-up canvas stool.

When they were at the rear of the Savoy Hotel, Cyril had heard this man, David Partiker, say to one of the Americans, 'My wife died last year.'

And here he is, saying it now to the Japs, 'My wife died last year.' A tiresome, self-absorbed little fellow.

'On we go,' Cyril calls.

He has omitted information about one of the murderers. Can't think which.

They regroup at number 55, Greek Street. In 1883, thirty-nine-year-old William Crees, prosperous harness maker, murdered Elizabeth Crees with a knife and a poker.

Frith Street. The Union Club. The Frenchman Charles Berthier murdered Charles Baladda. Money problems. Convicted, found insane.

Number 4 D'Arbly Street: 4th February 1856, William Bousfield walked into Bow Street Police Station. Agitated, shaking and covered in blood. Had killed his wife and three children.

The alleyway off Carnaby Street, the Blue Lagoon Club as it used to be. 1946, 91-year-old Charles Briginnorth murdered prostitute Margaret Cook.

Cyril Davenport, pain in his leg, dry as a dog, knows his lines, rattles them off, loudly for all the world to hear, his little entourage about him, out of breath, in a world of confusion. Debilitated.

Not much more to go now.

Lyon's Corner House Tearoom on the corner of Oxford Street and Tottenham Court Road. Recently taken over by Primark.

'Built in 1926, ladies and gentlemen, designed by FJ Wills, one of the best examples of the Beaux-Arts' style, of the late and eclectic form of Neoclassicism. On the 20th April 1945, outside this very building, which was erected on the site of the old Oxford Music Hall, Jacques Adrian Tratsart shot to death his father, sister, brother and himself. God knows, the poor deluded man, Jacques Adrian Tratsart, had had enough of life, enough of it all, ladies and gentlemen, the corruption, the inequality, the failures, the endless pain, the whole ghastly business. What was the point of it all?

Jacques Adrian Tratsart asked himself. God help him. What – was – the point?' Cyril cries out, his voice rising up the white faience façade, to the topmost third storey. Passers-by are staring. They are stepping aside and moving away. Two security officers emerge from inside the Primark store.

'Thank you, thank you, dear friends. That's it for today. Our guided tour has, alas, alas, come to an end.'

No sign of the Midlands folk. Strayed off. Slipped away. Not got the pertinacity. No sign of the Polish woman. He had forgotten about her. The Americans all present and correct. God bless America. He could have been big in America. He had at one time thought of going there to New York, LA, Hollywood. He had had the looks. God knows, many said that of him, that he had the looks, he had the trousers, he had the Moby Dick; it was the contacts one needed. Of course, it's always the same. No contacts, no fucking hope.

'Thank you for staying the course,' he says to the Americans, friends for life as, to him in his solitary state, they have become.

They'll sleep well tonight. Hotel, they say, in Paddington. Lord help them.

The two young ones from Hasting still here, laughing, laughing. Well, if it makes them happy. God knows he wished he could find it in himself to laugh like these young'uns, could find the hope that shines from their eyes, and them in bed fucking, with their boyfriends or whoever, man or woman; God, if he was only there again, back on tour, the Saturday nights, the hand taking his, a slight tug. It was always them, the women who led the way in these matters, who gave the green light, who took the decision and God bless them. But they are a long way off now, dead, some of them, cancer, heart, despair, some married money, a few of them celebrities in their own right. Lost touch now, such is the business. Such is life.

'That's it for today,' he says again. 'If you have enjoyed this tour, dear ladies and gentlemen, you may find it in yourselves this afternoon to show your appreciation.' Dear Heaven, does he have to spell it out? 'And those of you who are of a mind may wish to join me in a beverage or two at the Lamb and Flag which hostelry lies no further than a few minutes' walk, in Rose Street, a grand establishment, containing within its walls much of the history of our great European city. One of the oldest pubs in London and dates back to 1623. A long and rich history. Charles Dickens was himself a regular customer.'

'That was very, very interesting,' the American gent says.

He hands him a tenner.

'Ah, dear sir, how generous, how very good of you, and I do wish you good people, from the greatest nation on earth' – he's not going to get another tenner, he wonders why he bothers, but it's habit, it's in the blood, in the Max Factor, the greasepaint, it's the nine and five; ah, that's when we painted our faces, stage make-up – no one bothers now – unadorned faces, indistinguishable – 'I wish the three of you a continuingly enjoyable vacation in this our great City and, in due course, a safe journey home.'

The Americans are departing. Abandoning ship.

The Japs wave as they go. Waving not drowning. Lucky them, the little darlings. The young ones from Hastings are moving off towards Oxford Street Station, laughing.

David Partiker, the man on his own in the raincoat and hat and with the fold-up stool, remains.

'I'll join you if I may, at the Lamb and Flag,' he says.

David Partiker and Cyril Davenport in the Lamb and Flag, up at the bar. Each with a pint of London Pride. David Partiker's round, again.

'I was in The Mousetrap, you know,' Cyril says, directing the conversation safely to himself. 'Did I tell you I worked with that Gambon man, charming, very fine actor. Had a chat with him, in his dressing room. Called me over specially, over tea during a break in the filming.'

'Did you know the actress, Joan Blandingford?' David Partiker says.

Cyril on his fifth pint, David Partiker on his second.

'Joan Blandingford! God, did I know her? The craziest fucking actress known to man, and, by God, she was known to one helluva lot of 'man' was Joan; known by those in the know as 'Joan the head'. Make of that what you wish. Known by me, I have to say. Just the once or twice, once in a back alley off Westbourne Grove. Kept on talking, talking her head off during the event. God help us, chatter, chatter, chatter. Buggered up her career, in more ways than one, as we all know. Married to that fellow in insurance. Word had it,' he said – he desirous to inject a bit of fabricated drama into an occasion, and so fend off the ever- impending mundanity of life. 'the circumstances surrounding Joan Blandingford's demise were open to debate, if not to say decidedly fishy.

Such a show-off. Old Cyril. Eyes full of drink. Him with the cane, for all to behold. It'll not hold him as he and David Partiker reach the lights at the crossing from Long Acre to Cranbourn Street. It is of no help to him as he staggers and is propelled by David Partiker's fold-up canvas stool into the oncoming traffic.

A DAY AT THE CRICKET

Late afternoon, the Pavilion, Lord's Cricket Ground, Middlesex v. Surrey. Middlesex all out on 210 runs for 8 wickets.

Graham, Michael, Growly and David sitting alongside fellow MCC members; a number of whom they have known for some years, noticeably at Lord's, if not, by and large, in the world beyond; men in blazers, old school ties; the celebrated MCC ties with the egg and bacon stripes; grey slacks, black shoes, some brown. An overall predominance of greying hair.

The persistent and steady dismantling of Surrey's batsmen, the sound of ball on bat, the sudden cries of 'how's that?!'; the brief celebration on and off the pitch, players and spectators together, of a 4 to boundary, of a 6, a catch at silly-mid-on, a leg-before-wicket.

A helicopter overhead circling St John's Wood.

'A criminal at large, on the run,' someone along from them was heard to say.

The pain in Graham's right leg. His diabetes 2. The repeated resort to pain-killers, and his need to talk.

'My niece Annabelle,' Graham said to Michael, David and Growly. 'Her mother tells me she won't use the gender-neutral toilets at her sixth form college. All those boys in there making a nuisance of themselves. She tells me the girl, Annabelle holds it all in, won't pee when she ought to, and now she has a urine infection.'

A.J. Finch, batting for Surrey – a well-timed hook for a 4 to boundary.

'Aaron Finch is in good form. His third 4 in a row,' Michael said.

'He's looking for a half century,' Growly said.

'Gender neutral lavatories. Not all right, not at all,' Graham said. 'Not to my way of thinking. Those that they've got at my niece Annabelle's college; they are causing her all that trouble. A totally unsatisfactory arrangement, if you ask me. A chap goes in for a slash, goes in, stands there, pees down into the toilet, a chap tends to splash, tries not to, of course, but that's how we're made, standing there above the what's-it; bit of splash while you're standing there, knowing that any minute after you've left the place, a woman might well be coming in and there it is, bit of splash. Course, one would try to wipe it up, but, for fuck's sake, every time one goes to the lavatory for a pee one can't to be expected to lean down, bend over and clean the floor like a bloody domestic. Then there are those multi-purpose toilets. Unisex. Two or three cubicles. Have you been in one of them, Michael, Growly? Have you been in one of them, those unisex toilets, David? You're in there, you come out, there's a woman, a young woman, doing her makeup in the mirror by the wash basins. Of course, you try to remember to adjust your attire, as they used to say, but frankly I can't for the life of me believe any woman worth her salt wants a man to come out of the cubicle where he's been doing whatever he's doing and having him seeing her doing her make-up or whatever she's doing in the mirror, and him coming out hauling up his flies. God help us – it's the end of the fucking world. I said that to my wife, to Mary, about these new-fangled toilet arrangements. Splashing the floor and so on. She said perhaps I ought to sit down to have a pee like women do. No splashing, she said. I told her, you can't expect men to sit down, I said. Men aren't made that way. Look at dogs, I said to her; the female, the bitch goes down on her rear legs to pee. The male dog lifts his leg. Stands by the tree or lamp post and lifts his leg. It's nature. You can't change nature. Men have to pee standing up. Up. Not at a lamppost of course; well, only if and when caught short and too far from the requisite facilities. Sitting down, I tell her, tell my wife Mary, and we won't be able to do it. Nothing would happen. We'd sit there and nothing would occur. Mary says she's read that German men sit on the toilet when they pee. I said to her, no wonder they lost the war.

'There goes Aaron Finch, caught at wicket,' Growly said.
'Out for 47,' Graham said.

'I'm changing the flowers on Joan's grave today,' David said.
God help us, don't let's go down that road again, Graham thought. The chap's wife died a year ago, very sorry and all that, everyone sympathises. But the man never stops going on about it. Here I am, telling them about Annabelle and these new-fangled toilet arrangements, there's Sam Curran, hitting another splendid four, and out of the blue, out of nowhere David Partiker starts on about his deceased wife again. The sky above is a glorious British azure blue, and there he is, in his beige rain hat and raincoat, holding out against the possibility of rain, for God's sake; there he is, bringing misery to an otherwise pleasant enough day at the

cricket by going on about his wife Joan again, telling everyone that later today he is planning to lay flowers on the woman's grave. Best ignored. As always. Don't encourage him. Change the subject fast.

David Partiker, as Graham, Michael and Growly have known for some time, was retired; worked for many years in Insurance. Physical health good. Some arthritis. His wife's passing, to all intents and purposes, had left him at a complete loss.

'Ah, yes, a difficult time for you, David. Our sympathies, old chap,' Michael said.

Good old Michael. If in a fix, get Michael on board. Part of his success in life and business. Genial Michael. A natural. Tax accountant. Good chap to know.

'I didn't think much of Archie's funeral,' Graham said.

Archie's death and funeral have been spoken of before.

'I'd have thought that Archie would have gone on for a good few more years yet,' Growly said.

Away from the cricket 'Growly' was the actors' agent Dennis Barker of Dennis Barker Personal Management. Sporting a fierce MCC tie at Lord's, with his bristle beard and his misleadingly sombre countenance, his fellow cricket enthusiasts had accorded him the nickname 'Growly'.

'What are these actors like?' Graham had at one time asked him.

'Children. Greedy insecure little sods,' Growly had said. He loved every single one of them. They paid the bills, he'd said.

Growly was thinking now, as he had been thinking from time to time that day, of Roger Marchmant, actor, one of his clients, knocked off his perch, cancer. Bloody cancer. It was the same with Julie, Julie Randerson, high earner. Julie, lovely sweet uncomplaining Julie. Got cancer, she said one day. Came in to the office. Unexpectedly. But welcome. Julie would always be welcome. Got cancer, she said to him. God, sorry to hear that, he'd said. So bloody sorry, he had said to Julie. Six months. Six bloody months and she'd gone. Off the books. God bless the woman.

'Sam Curran out. Caught at wicket,' Graham said.
'Out for 39,' Michael said.

'Those people at Archie's funeral. Didn't recognize half of them,' Graham said, the pain in his blasted right leg playing up.

It was the diabetes, that was the cause of it; that was his GP's explanation. Not that one should ever trust the word of a bloody GP. Jack of all trades, master of none. That was Graham's opinion. Bloody GP tells him he has to stop smoking, bloody man leaning over his fucking computer, tapping away like he's writing a bloody novel, and tells him to give up smoking and he's already given it up, for God's sake, gave it up two years ago, hadn't he, the stupid bastard.

'Archie; he was a good chap,' he said. 'A one-off.'

They'd all known Archie from cricket at Lords, and at the Hurlingham Club.

'Archie was a good chap all in all,' Graham said again. 'An old fool when it came to women. Made a small fortune from commercial property, but women, God help him, he buggered up there. Didn't know women. Thought he did. He didn't. That was Archie. Three wives. The last one took him for four hundred and seventy-five thousand quid. Archie's eightieth birthday party. That woman Carrie was there. She'd lined herself up as Archie's fourth.'

'If she had had her way,' Michael said.

'If she had had her way,' Growly said.

'If she had had her way,' David said.

'Carrie; portrait painter, or so she has claimed; portrait paintings of a horrid burnt orange hue. God, no one has a complexion that colour, only in Carrie's paintings,' Graham said. 'She had her hooks into Archie. That was for certain.'

It seemed to Graham, and to those who had known Archie, that, uncharacteristically, when it came to Carrie and marriage, this boat owning, commercial property owner, this sporty tennis player and member of the RAC Club had been vacillating. It had seemed he had felt it was something he shouldn't rush into, that he ought to give it some serious thought. It had been expected, however, that, in the fullness of time, the Carrie woman would no doubt have managed to have hauled him in. But before she could, the bugger had died of heart failure.

'I had lunch with Archie at Browns,' Graham said. 'A couple of weeks before he died. It was that second wife of his, Margaret, who did it for him. He never got over that. Archie bought her a house in Italy.'

They had heard it all before.

'Archie bought her a house in Italy. Then the bitch gave him his cards. No explanation. Told him he couldn't visit her out there in Italy. Changed her phone number. The woman's mad, that's what Archie said. Told me she needed to see a psychiatrist,' Graham said, the pain in his right leg beyond bearing.

He reached into his blazer pocket for the bottle of painkillers he'd been prescribed. Swallowed two with water from his bottle of Evian. Not that they did any good. But every now and again, he'd take a couple. Keep talking, that was the thing to do. There had been a time when the cricket had been enough to distract him from the pain. But no longer.

'That's it,' Growly said. 'Rikki Clarke's out. Caught mid-wicket by Ab de Villiers.'
'Out for a single,' Graham said.
'Nice ball from Steve Finn,' Growly said.

Michael was checking a text on his phone.
'From Rebecca, from your wife?' Graham said.
'Yes. She's in Gothenburg, in Sweden. Anthropological seminar.'
'I thought it was Estonia,' Growly said.
'Yes, it was. Now she's in Sweden. She says she's just been invited to speak at an anthropological event in Ljubljana, Slovenia.'
'She's very much in demand,' David said.

'Do you go to the theatre much?' Graham said to Growly.
'Not if I can help it,' Growly said.
'Mary and I went to that play at the National, this was awhile ago,' Graham said to Growly, whom he considered an authority on matters theatrical. 'A play about a boy's public school in the 1950's. I was at the same school as the author, you know. Not at the same time of course; more recently; quite a few years after him of course. The play didn't have anything about cricket in it. No cricket in it at all. The school he and I went to, it was cricket, cricket all the time. Everyone passionate about cricket. No mention of cricket in the play. None at all.'
'Well, the school in the play was fiction in a way, wasn't it?' Growly said.
'Yes, yes, of course. I know. But he didn't mention cricket in his play, not once.'

'Do you go to the theatre much, David?' he said.

'Not now Joan's gone,' David said. 'Joan loved the theatre. It was in her blood, you know.'

'Of course,' Michael said.

'Wonderful actress,' Graham said.

'She was in her element on stage, in a movie. Well, we all know that,' David said. 'Couldn't have enough of it, one way or another. She was relentless. I said to her, Joan, darling, you're relentless. What I meant was she was driven, dedicated. Not relentless. I oughtn't to have used the word relentless. But there you are. Relentless. She knew me as D.P, you know. My initials. David Partiker. Of course. This is D.P. she'd say to her friends. My husband D.P, she'd say. Only, some of her friends got it wrong and pronounced it 'Dippy'. Hello, Dippy, they'd say. I'd say no, that's not quite correct, but they didn't seem to understand, kept calling me Dippy. But then, so did Joan. Dippy darling, see you later tonight, see you in three weeks after we've finished the movie. She was always so busy; the theatre, movies, the great love of her life.'

'4! Good shot. Past 3rd man for a 4,' Michael said.

'Nice bit of batting from Jordan Clark,' Graham said.

'I've always preferred it when plays were in three acts, Growly,' Graham said. 'Nowadays it's two, even one. Not any good for theatre bar takings I'd have thought. Used to be three. That was the normal. Half an hour. Interval, drinks in the bar; gin and tonic for Mary; Scotch or beer for me. Second act; thirty minutes, the drama or the comedy reaches a peak. Interval. Drinks. Gin and tonic, Scotch or beer. Third Act; 30 minutes. The killer arrested. Resolution. We like matinees now. The actors seem to get through it quicker. Come out about half five, get a spot of early dinner; one of the Italian places. Back home in time for the News at Ten. I like her, don't you? What's her name? Pretty face, does the Antiques show. Taken over the wretched Question Time. She'd have done well to keep clear of that. Politicians and self-centred know-alls coming out with the same old gumf. The three-act play; a thing of the past. And sometimes, there are plays that last about twenty minutes. Twenty minutes. I mean, you pay out good money. You pay out good money, and you're out in the street before you have had time to get settled. Bloody nonsense. Twenty minutes. Friends of ours, top man at British Telecom and his wife, went to see one of them, one of the twenty-minute sort, couldn't make head or tale of it. Convoluted rubbish. In that place in Sloane Square.'

Graham reached into his blazer pocket for the pain killers. He swallowed two with the water.

'Bloody leg,' he said. 'I've got an ulcer. Mary's cooking me what she calls special meals. Chicken, fish, vegetables, brown rice, fruit and yogurt.'

'You don't deserve her,' Growly said.

'I'm having to cut down on the beer,' Graham said.

He wasn't giving up. There was always the cricket. A day at the cricket, with Growly, Michael, and even with David, as long as the latter would desist from going on and on about his late wife all the fucking time.

'The vicar at Archie's funeral,' he said. 'I didn't know what he was talking about. Did you, Michael? It wasn't Archie at all. Not the one we know. His love of gardening? Never heard Archie say he was interested in gardening. A family-man? Christ. And how many families? Three wives. Two kids. One in Australia, the other in 'God-knows-where'. That fellow at the funeral who read that poem. Professor type. Who was he? Anyone know?'

'No idea,' Michael said.

'He took his time, didn't he? With the poem. He couldn't find it, could he? I said to Mary, he's lost it. The poem. It's in his shoulder bag; he's lost it, I said to her. Couldn't hear a word he read of it. Couldn't hear him. You were lucky not to be there, Growly. Couldn't understand a word he uttered. I thought he'd had a stroke. God only knows how Archie came to know him. Fucking inaudible. The poem from Eliot. Waste Lands. Archie and Eliot. Give me a break. If it had been Betjeman, that might have made sense. Archie wasn't any sort of poetry enthusiast, not as far as I know. Archie, if pressed, might go for Raymond Chandler, Jeffrey Archer, James Patterson. Not fucking Eliot.'

'Jade Dernbach, Ben Foakes – not a run between them for the past five minutes,' Michael said.

'Tony Roland-Jones' has got them on the back foot,' Growly said.

'Him and Steve Finn between them,' Graham said.

'I took the train to Rochester last week,' David said.

'Attractive town, Rochester. A lot of Dickens in Rochester. He lived at Gad's Hill Place,' Michael said.

'It was the first anniversary of Joan's passing,' David said. 'I took the train from St Pancras.'

One year to the day of Joan's death, David had been looking out of their bedroom window in their house in North London. He had gone downstairs, out of the front door. Walked to the gate, onto the pavement, up the street, not at all sure where he was going, but keeping going, which was what he felt he had to do, he walked up the hill to the shops in the street, his blue-blazered upper body stooped, his short legs in his grey flannels pushing forward, one then the other, as if with some effort, past the cinema in the street, past the fish, the meat, the charity shops, took the Tube to St Pancras, thinking he'd take the train to Rochester. Joan had been fond of Rochester. There was that restaurant which Joan had liked very much. He'd go to Rochester and have lunch there, he thought. When he got to St Pancras, he had a coffee in Starbucks. He looked at the holiday pages in a newspaper someone had left behind on the table. Advertisements for cruises. There were so many cruises, everyone's going on cruises, he thought. There were advertisements for ten days in the Dordogne. A colourful picture in an advert' for Havana. Seven days in Cuba. From £1049. Four-star hotel, room only. He'd never been to Cuba. He thought Joan would have loved to live for a time in Havana, among its faded paintwork, derelict buildings, iron balconies, its unstable history. That was Joan. Its mystery, its poverty even. He saw himself there with Joan, in their favourite café-bar, to be welcomed with a familiar nod and smile, an acceptance, to play Cubilete with Mendo and Emeterio, with young Juaneta Perera serving the Pian Colado and the obligatory glass of water. He was uncertain of his facts. He thought he had at one time read a book about Cuba. A book by Graham Greene, he seemed to remember. It would be six in the evening in Havana, and at nine, in the company of Graham Greene, they'd drift down the street to the rooms they'd rented from the Klevansky's in Calle Lamparilla.

'What's that book about Cuba by Graham Green called?' he now asked his MCC companions.

'Our Man in Havana,' Growly and Michael said.

He had taken the train to Rochester but the restaurant she'd liked had been closed. It had been a Monday. He'd walked up the narrow High Street with its clothes shops, and visited the Cathedral, and the Castle. He'd caught the open top tourist bus to Gillingham and Chatham. An audio tape called attention to places of historical interest. Then he'd come home. He had taken her nightgown from her chest of drawers, and had slept the night with it at his side.

'Gosh, it's slow out there,' Michael said of the match.

'Need a walk. Need a pee. Walk the bloody leg,' Graham said as he hauled himself up onto his feet.

Growly thought he'd not stay, not go to the Members' bar for a beer after the game. He'd get home to his wife Carol in their house in North Finchley, home for egg and chips. It was always egg and chips after a day at Lords.

'Have you had anything to eat, Podgy?' Carol would ask him.

'No.'

'Egg and chips.'

'Lovely.'

She called him Podgy. That was her name for him. Podgy at home, Growly at Lords, Dennis Barker at the office.

He'd sit himself in his armchair in their large living room overlooking their summer garden, and settle down with *The Times* until Carol called 'egg and chips' which they'd eat in the kitchen. Then it would be TV and bed.

'We're going to have to find a new gardener, Podgy. Bruce is going back to Canada,' Carol said to him last night.

She'd come in from the garden.

'Podgy, we're going to have to find a new gardener,' she said.

She went back to the garden and soon came in again.

'Podgy, dear, can you drive me down to the Garden Centre tomorrow, I need to buy a verbena and some gloves and some of that grease for the apple trees.'

'Maybe I should retire, chuck it in,' he said.

'Don't be daft, Podgy, darling,' she said to him. 'What would you do with yourself? There're only so many days you can spend watching the cricket. I can't have you hanging around the house doing nothing. Anyway, you love it.'

Later that evening they watched one of his clients in a spy series on Sky.

'I think it's time I retired,' he said.

It was a hard-nosed bloody business. The fun had gone out of it. More competition. It was a young person's game.

'Why does everything on tele have to be so violent these days?' Carol said.

'That's the second car crash in thirty seconds. Your chap hasn't got so much to do this week, has he?'

He was respected, was Dennis. Considered a wizard with contracts, at negotiations. A bit slow at seeking opportunities.

'There's not so much of your chap this week,' Carol said.

Graham was not yet back from having a pee.

Growly was thinking that maybe he should hand over the agency to his associate Stephie. He and Carol were comfortably off. He could spend more time with the grandchildren. Stephie was on top of her game. He liked her. Carol liked her. She was the best. And Jane in the office was solid, loyal, been with him all of fifteen years. Jane knew the business, dealt with the enquiries, sorted out the problems.

When he had started in the late eighties, the agency had been one room above a shoe shop in Great Marylebone Street. No secretary then. A room the size of a cupboard. One desk, phone, built-in shelves, filing cabinet he bought from behind St Pancras Station. Took on anybody. People liked him. Young Dennis was dependable. Thirty years later, he had an office in Mayfair, had a large detached house in North Finchley, and his and Carol's place in Tuscany. Worked three days a week in the office and two days from home. Then there was the cricket. Lords. His escape-hole, as Carol has said.

Graham was on his way back, awkwardly negotiating the row of seats.

'Surrey's going down like nine pins,' Growly said.

'It's not their day,' Michael said.

Graham felt in his blazer pocket for the bottle of pain killers. He felt, and left them there. He didn't want to turn into a fucking drug addict.

'Finn nearly got Ben Foakes,' Michael said. 'I thought he'd got him there. Looked like LBW to me.'

'Archie's first wife Penelope had mental health issues,' Graham said. 'Did you know that? Archie told me. We were having lunch at Browns. Steak and Guinness pie, bottle of Cave De Fleurie Beaujolais, Brown's apple and rhubarb crumble. Ten days before he died. Before he copped it. She had anxiety issues, he said. Went for a few weeks, an inpatient, or whatever they call them nowadays, in a Private Clinic. According to Archie she played ping pong. They had a ping pong table. And she did Yoga.'

'Joan did yoga for a time,' David said.

'Oh good,' Graham said.

'Dog yoga,' David said. 'She bought a dog, a Yorkshire Terrier, did Yoga with it. Put it on her back. Knelt down, put it on her back, did Yoga. Joan and the dog.'

'Good show,' Michael says.

'Could be money in it,' Growly said.

'That's what Joan said,' David said.

'Anyway,' Graham said, God help him, he wished the chap would give over about Joan, her doing yoga or whatever it was with a fucking dog, 'Archie's wife Penelope went to this private clinic where they did morning walks, pottery classes, and Self Esteem Group Therapy. Archie said she and the rest of them had to go around saying, "Hello, everybody. Look at me, aren't I simply adorable." She had to see this bloody psychiatrist. The psychiatrist fellow charged her two hundred quid for fifty minutes. He turned up half an hour late, had her fill in a depression inventory. The man told her she wasn't bad enough to be an in-patient. He said she ought to go on a day-centre programme that was going to cost her one hundred and seventy-five quid a day. She told him to fuck off.

Michael was on his phone.

'Texting Rebecca,' Michael said. 'Bringing her up to date with the match.'

'Surrey's looking for a defeat,' Growly said.

'On the back foot, playing it safe,' Graham said.

'Our son Josh and his wife Sarah are supposed to be coming over with the grandchildren, Sunday,' Michael said. 'We were hoping to have a bit of a celebration, Rebecca's home-coming.'

'She'll be back soon,' Graham said.

It had been Archie who introduced Michael to Rebecca. At the Hurlingham. Tennis; a doubles match. 'Got a partner for you,' Archie had said to him. 'Rebecca. Watch out for her back hand.' Rebecca: tall, slim, athletic. Brunette. 'You've got me to thank for introducing you to her,' Archie had said. Said more than the once. Pleased as punch with himself, he'd been.

She'd never been interested in cricket. He took her to Lords when they first met, showed her the Long Room. After they were married, he asked her if she wanted to come to the MCC Club Dinner. 'You could meet Mike Gatting,' he said. 'Mike Gatting's going to be there.' 'What the blazes are you talking about?' she said. And then 'All right, I'll come,' she said.

The MCC Club Dinner; the Long Room packed. Men in black tie, ladies in Biba, Rick Owens, House of Fraser. Rebecca in a Lauren Ralph Lauren long blue maxi dress. Archie there; Graham and his wife Mary, Growly and his wife Carol, David and his Joan. Joan, putting on an act, playing the star, in a grey-green open-back satin maxi-dress. Tall, slim, red hair. Something of the Irish about her, Michael thought. Archie flirting with her. Inappropriate, that had been Michaels' opinion, although he hadn't said. Rumour had it, that one time in the small hours of the night Joan had been found wandering around Covent Garden wearing nothing more than a raincoat and a pair of ballet pumps.

Graham's Mary there at the MCC dinner in a long, green dress. Sensible woman. Senior lecturer in Humanities at a North East London College. Took early retirement. Michael heard her telling

Graham to stand up straight. Pulled at his dinner jacket to try to make him look less lopsided.

Archie and Joan openly flirting. Having the time of their lives. David at the table, sitting there as if he was watching a performance.

A few years ago, Growly had had a phone call at the office from David's wife, Joan. Would he be her agent? Fed up with her present one. Joan was unreliable. Had a reputation. More trouble than she was worth. Growly had told her he was sorry, the agency wasn't taking on any new clients. Had told Jane in the office not to put her through to him should she phone again. Never heard any more about it from her. He'd not said anything about it to David.

'Do you remember Jack Williston?' Graham said. 'Archie told me he'd got Kim Kardashian tattooed on his penis. That's what Archie heard. I rather expect it was just her initials. KK. On his penis. Not the whole woman. I don't know much about Jack Williston, but I greatly doubt he could get all of Kim Kardashian on there. An attractive woman, no doubt about it, but nevertheless. I rather think at Jack Williston's age, one has quite enough to put up with vis-à-vis one's nether regions without having yourself tattooed. Frankly, I hate the bloody things, tattoos. Don't like them. You see them, on these women, young women, perfectly good young women, youth, some of them lovely, I'll say it myself – blooming lovely – and they vandalize themselves with this god-damn awful graffiti. Thing is, when they get older, get over 50, 60, get to our ages, well, mine anyway, what then? Eh? What will those tattoos, the arms, backs, legs, God-knows-where, look like then? It doesn't bear thinking about. You see them – I've seen them, have you, Michael, Growly?

Scribbled all over. Big red and black blotches. You look at some of them, you think, I think, where are you? What have you done? – neck, chest, chest – across the chest; then there's the piercing, the ears, the nose; nose piercings hanging from the nose, like snot. Going around, walking around, perfectly decent looking young women with snot hanging from their noses, for Christ's sake. Are they mad? Piercings and tattoos and God-knows-what things they've done to themselves.'

'Joan had a tattoo,' David said. 'On her back.'

'Tom Helm to Imran Tahir. Got him! All out for 146,' Michael said.

'That's it!' Growly said. 'All over. Home team wins by 64 runs!'

Sweet Caroline rung out across the ground, the crowd in good voice, giving it all they'd got, Graham. Michael, Growly and David belting it out with the best of them.

* *

That Autumn, Michael's wife Rebecca returned home to England and she and Michael moved to Croxley Green, Hertfordshire.

Graham had a stroke which paralysed him down his right side and left him unable to speak.

David Partiker was seen in a village in Norfolk which his late wife Joan had loved to visit. He was wearing Joan's autumn green woollen dress, her red winter overcoat and four-inch heels.

Dennis Barker, known at Lord's as Growly and at home as Podgy, celebrated his and Carol's 30th wedding anniversary with their children and their families. They had the living room in their house in North Finchley, London, refurbished. Upholstery by Colefax and Fowler, the walls in elephant grey; Carol's choice.

KINGS CROSS

It was memories of better days mostly that served to sustain Claire. Memories of Wharton Street where she used to work with James and Sheila, Teddy, Bill, and Chloe, on the TV documentaries; family friendly, most of which never saw the light of day. But then, that was the business. Some were made, some weren't. At that time there had been the long boozy work lunches at L'Oranger. Later, after she retired, she had continued to meet up with a handful of old friends at the Tandoori in Kings Cross. And now that the lunches were no more, had not been for some time, no one being available, or so it would seem, it was the memories of them and of those who had come along, those whom she had known, and the years in Wharton Street.

There had been Johnny but Johnny was gone. Steve had Parkinson's. Beth was in Portugal with a man called Tip, whom Claire couldn't rightly remember, him not being one of the old crowd. There had been Martin, of course. He had been her main man, well, on and off, for almost five years. Then he'd met that woman and they'd gone to live in Brazil.

She had come to dreadfully miss the social interaction which to her was always an imperative.

It had become Facebook and Instagram mostly for Claire

now. Daily posts, four, five times a day, fishing out old photos of the gang at Wharton Street, at L'Oranger. Of the conference in Barbados, the beach, the cocktails. It was Dickie there, just the one night. Dickie was fine. Nice man, wife and three little kids; but Barbados and cocktails, and the midnight swim in the hotel pool, well, it was Dickie whose hand she had taken, gently, and it was Dickie till sunrise when he dispatched himself to his own room, with the parting words of appreciation. 'Very nice', he had said. It was 'photies' of Amsterdam for the Wortleton shoot, there they all were, broad smiles, bleary eyed after the launch. She couldn't recall the launch, what it was for, but there were the 'photies' on her FB page. Along with posts about her eyesight, about her GP, her meds, her walks, the park, the houses off the High Road. Enquiries, observations. 'Am I right in saying…?' 'Is anyone having trouble with…?' 'My water bill came this a.m. …' 'God. I hate these electric scooters…'

Some days, she had to confess, it felt as if, when things were quiet and the emulsion white walls of her flat stared dispassionately back at her, it was FB where she could be found, where, it seemed, she mostly resided.

Then Jackson phoned. Jackson, 'the straw that broke the camel's back'. Not heard from or seen for how long? Six, eight years? Then he phones. She was pleased, of course. She thought she was pleased. She felt she ought to feel pleased. It was, after all, Jackson. Six feet two, broad shoulders. He'd be seventy-three or thereabouts, she thought. Good, very good in bed. He was probably good now. But too late. She had given all that up a long, long time ago. Or so she seemed to remember.

'I'm coming to see you,' he said.

'Lunch. The Italian,' she said.

'My treat,' he said.

'You bet yer,' she replied.

The Italian. Lunch. Quite like the old days. Only without Steve and Beth, and all those others. It was just Jackson, who at one time was good in bed, but what was the use of that now?

'Darling. How lovely,' she said, and reached up, gave his right cheek a kiss. Left her lipstick on it, in a smudge. Wiped it off with her fingers. Quick. All gone. And he gave her a hug. Like the old days. Only not like. Not now. Now it was almost a business-like hug, and a broad, mutually shared grin, a sense of, well, thank goodness we've got the preliminaries over and done with. And inside the Italian they went.

It had not been like it used to be; a hug, a kiss, the expectation of sex later. Later they would have had sex. He had been good at it, she reminded herself. She too had been pretty hot stuff. People had said so. They themselves had heard it said by those who had had direct evidence of it. Such recognition had always been important to her. After sex, she had left Jackson 'glowing as in the early morning summer's day'. He had said so. He was a man for words.

'I feel like a king,' he'd say.

Of course, he was a bastard. Of course. So? Who wasn't? It had been cut throat. That had been part of the fun. That's how it had been at Wharton Street. No holds barred. And she had been the champion, held her own, unlike some, unlike Josie who went under, threw herself beneath the 8.45 Central Line train, causing those delays; so selfish, she had said, people keen to get to work.

After lunch at L' Oranger, she and Jackson would go back to his place in Swinton Street. What a mess, that flat of his. But she had barely noticed. Lunch over, the others had gone. Half three. It had been she and him.

'Hello, Dan.'

They were in the Italian. Jackson had phoned, and here they were in the Italian at the table near the back and opposite the toilets.

'Hello, Dan,' the fella said.

He came over, on his way out, stopped by the table, looked down at her, then at Jackson. People had always looked at her before looking at anyone else, she remembered.

'Hello, Dan,' he said.

Jackson raised a hand.

The fella, whoever he was, walked off and left the premises.

So now she was sitting with Jackson, who was not Jackson. Not anymore. He was Dan.

'Who's this Dan?' she said.

'Oh, that's nothing,' he said.

'Nothing?'

'Some people, well, a few, know me as Dan.'

'Dan?'

'Yep.'

'I prefer Jackson.'

'No problem,' he said.

No problem? Was he Dan or was he Jackson way back then in the blue beyond when they, when she and he – pardon the expression she would say – were 'getting it on' in Swinton Street?

'Is this recent?' she said. 'This change of name. This dual identity?' Have you gone completely mad? Don't you know who you are?'

Jackson was not as she had known him. It was as if he was no more, didn't exist, hadn't existed. She had lost friends, all those friends and, unexpectedly, here was Jackson from those old days, and he wasn't. He wasn't Jackson. He was God-knows-who. He was someone called Dan.

It wasn't as if he had changed gender, gone under the knife, become Paula or Marianne. She could have understood that. In the present climate that would have been no longer so out of the ordinary. What about Len who worked at the pub off the Caledonian Road? Now big mighty Len was big bulky Marjorie. These changes, it seemed to her, were becoming almost as common, as every day, as facelifts, as breast implants and tummy tucks.

He hated the name Jackson, he said. Had always hated it. Blamed his parents. But how were they to know? she thought. He was in transition, he said. It was for him a gradual 'ting', he said. He was Irish, Dublin. It had been part and parcel of his attraction – women liked his voice, the way he put words together, sentences, the cool lyrical tune to him.

He was getting to the point now, more and more each day that passed, he said to her during their second bottle of the House Merlot, where he would be able to offload Jackson altogether and be free to be Dan.

It was everywhere now, she thought. People were dissatisfied with whom they were, with whom they thought people thought them to be; joining this group, that movement, allying themselves with a cause, a political standpoint, a set of beliefs, dogma, righteous outrage; looking for the means to secure a semblance of an identity they could internalize and with which they could armour themselves. It reminded her of EST. EST, the fad, the human potential movement, back in the 70's; go on a course of EST, come out confident, unassailable. Only, it didn't work, not with George, went to his head, his eyes staring fanatically, crashing into walls of resistance.

After the Italian with Dan there she was back at her flat, in front of the television at four in the afternoon watching quizzes, game shows, antique road trips, the occasional old movie. A sad bitch, that's me, she said to herself. There she was on Face Book, on Instagram, posting every day, what she had had for breakfast, pictures of her new glasses, pictures of her wearing the glasses, pictures of her with friends and associates from times past, with friends in towns and cities where they'd been on work and on holiday, pictures of the evening sky, of a sunrise, the next door's cat on the fence, the back of the Amazon delivery man, as she thanked him. She hauled photos out of boxes, albums, of old times, old friends. L' Oranger, Wharton Street, Barbados again, London Bridge with Sally, poor dear Sally over at London Bridge. Lost her job, lost her bloke. Picture there of Sally, looking fabulous.

Then there was Lyn on FB. She was an FB friend, although Claire couldn't for the life of her think who she was. But there was someone called Lyn posting her depression, her cries of 'Why do I go on?' Someone had died and she wouldn't get over it. It was all very depressing, Lyn's depression, her depressing posts. Claire hoped she would have 'liked' the pictures she had posted of her new glasses, of her wearing the glasses. But Lyn hadn't seemed to know who the hell she was.

Claire decided 'enough was enough'. She would organize another of her lunches. They hadn't had one for ages. She had got out of the habit. One had to move on, she said to herself. She had to 'take the bull by the horns'.

She messaged half a dozen of those in her old WhatsApp group whom she wished to invite. 'Thursday, 2 o'clock. The Italian. After the city workers have gone back to work, I've spoken with the restaurant. All planned. Dan's coming. Do let me know if you can come so I can make sure we have the right size table.'

Dan couldn't come. He emailed her. 'Sorry, have an appointment with the bank.'

Dan wasn't coming. But Peter and Barry, and Chloe – she had messaged them and Josh, although she wasn't sure she hadn't heard that Josh was dead, died in Athens. Michael would come, she was sure of that. There'd be six of them. Not bad after all that time.

They knew her at the Italian. They had laid out a table for six at the back near the kitchens. She arrived on time. She had always been on time. Punctuality was one of her boasts.

'They'll be here soon,' she said to the waiter, a nice young Italian.

She ordered a Martini to start things off. Browsed the menu. She hadn't needed to. She had seen it so many times. She knew what she wanted. Baked Lasagne.

She sipped her Martini.

She began to speak with Peter. Although Peter wasn't there. Then Chloe. Dear, darling Chloe, after all this time, those wonderful years at Wharton Street, and in Antigua for the shoot. 'Darling, how lovely,' Claire said, giving Chloe, who was not there, a friendly nudge. That's what they did in the old days, gave each other a nudge when during one of their weekly Wharton Street meetings someone or other made a suggestion which on numerous occasions had already been turned down and consigned to the litter bin.

'We're waiting for Josh and Michael,' she said to the young waiter. 'Won't be long,' she said.

'Michael, he's dreadful, he's never on time,' she said to Chloe and Peter. 'Oh, look, who's here? It's Barry. Barry's here,' she said. 'Shall we order? I'm having the Baked Lasagne.'

'I always have the Baked Lasagne,' she said to the young Italian waiter.

Dan arrived.

'Dan!'

The appointment with the bank had been cancelled, he said. So, here he was.

'Anyone else coming?' he said.

'Maybe they'll turn up later,' she said.

Michael arrived.

'Lost my way here,' he said.

'You always have done, Michael,' Claire said.

'Hi,' Chloe called.

'Chloe,' Claire called. 'Come and sit next to me.'

And Chloe did. For Chloe was there, as was Dan and Michael, and soon after, Peter, who'd put on weight, and Josh who wasn't dead after all, and they all had a lovely time of it, just like the old days, they said, when they were at Wharton Street, and have you heard about… and my goodness, the world's gone crazy, utterly mad… the Linguine Mare is delicious, I forgot how delicious it was. We must do this again. Well done, Claire, great idea.

'Cheers, everyone.'

Glasses clinked.

STRANDED IN BRISTOL

'There's mucus all down the back of my throat, Bryn,' Gwyneth said.

She rose and walked unsteadily across the room. She leant over Bryn, who was sitting on the edge of the bed.

'Can you see anything?' she said, her mouth wide open.

'Where?' he asked.

'I saw something like a lump.'

That morning Gwyneth Pearce-Williams was sitting under the window of Room 37 in the Bellingham Hotel in Bristol.

The previous evening in the Colston Hall, accompanied by her pianist Bryn, she had given her recital of songs from operettas and popular musicals.

It was a standard hotel room, a bed, a bedside table, a door leading to the ensuite bathroom. Gwyneth's two suitcases were in a corner, Bryn's suitcase was waiting at the door. Bryn's right hand was heavily bandaged.

Outside it was raining heavily.

'We have to vacate the hotel in half an hour,' Bryn said. 'They're cleaning my room already.'

She opened her mouth wider for him to make a closer examination. Gwyneth was ill at ease and fretful in the mornings, and her face, now close to his, mirrored her state of mind. At that time of day, she found it too much of an effort to conjure up the charm which she was able to produce when, on the concert platform, she was standing before her audience, her blonde hair framing her face and her smile ever bright and eager.

In 'the good old days', when she had been at the height of her career, there had been an occasion when Bryn had thought he would have quite liked to have had sex with Gwyneth. That had been during their tour of Ayrshire, Arran and the Highlands. He had known of course that, had he propositioned her, she would have rebuffed his advances. So, always anxious not to invite rejection, he hadn't.

'I can't see a lump,' he said.

'There's something there,' she said.

She went back to the chair by the window.

'I'll try Vic on the phone again in a few minutes,' Bryn said. 'He's only popped out for a moment. He says so – his voice mail.'

'My God, you make me sick, Bryn,' she complained. 'We're in the last few weeks of this insufferable tour. We've a recital in Liverpool this evening. And you have to get drunk, fall over and break your wrist.'

'I wasn't drunk,' he said.

'You could hardly stand up. When we came out of that pub, you were reeling.'

'It was the carpet downstairs in the hall,' he said.

'Blame it on the hotel, won't you? A bloody pianist with a broken wrist.'

'It's not broken. It's sprained,' he said.

'You can't play the piano though, can you? We've a recital in Liverpool in six hours!'

'I'll try Vic again in a couple of minutes,' he said.

'I don't want Vic. He thumps. Bang, bang, bang. Bang, bang, bang. A night with him, I feel as if I've been through fifteen rounds with Mike Tyson,' she said.

She clasped her aching throat. Bryn was hopeless. He was spineless. She might have thought better of him if he didn't always insist on wearing that green tweed jacket and those appalling blue cords. She had told him he ought to wear something else, but, to her, it was all too apparent he couldn't find it in himself to do so. He was as he was. And he being who he was, more than anything else, was what annoyed Gwyneth the most.

'What time's the train?' she asked.

'Twelve seventeen. They're expecting us at four thirty. You think I should phone Gerald to ask him to stand in for me?' he said.

'No!' she snapped.

'He's a wonderful pianist. You never had a better accompanist, Gwyneth.'

'I am never ever working with Gerald Jenkins again,' she cried out. 'We were married fifteen years. I make a home for him. And he walks out, goes off with that Pauline Ellis woman with the Royal Philharmonic. That bloody cello wedged between her legs. Then Pauline Ellis goes off with the first violin. And bloody Gerald goes off with Branwen Roberts with her harp. What he sees in Branwen Roberts and her harp I cannot imagine.'

'We've got to find someone, Gwyneth,' he said, attempting to appeal to her common sense.

'I'm not working with Gerald, Bryn,' she said. She was adamant. Intractable.

She didn't know why she agreed to do these tours. She had told her agent she deserved better. The agent had said work was scarce these days. It was easy for her to say that, sitting in her office and not having to budge an inch, not having to tolerate the travelling, the car journeys, the hotel rooms, the lack of consideration and cooperation.

Why couldn't it be the same as it used to be when she toured all over Europe?

'My lips are all swollen, Bryn,' she said.

She stuck her tongue in and out, to the left and to the right and straight ahead.

'My tongue, Bryn. It's not working, for God's sake.'

'I'll phone Vic again,' he said.

He picked up his phone from the bed and dialled.

'There's a lump there. I'm sure I can see a lump,' she said, looking at her throat in her hand mirror.

'He's still not there,' Bryn said, ringing off.

The rain could be heard beating against the window.

'I suppose it's sort of like Waiting for Godot,' Bryn said.

'What?'

'Waiting for Godot. It's like us.'

'What is?'

'It just occurred to me. There are these men. They're waiting. For Godot,' he said.

'What for?'

'Well, it's difficult to say. It's a play.'

'A play, is it?'

'Yes. You heard about it?'

'A play? No.'

'Only, it just came to me, it's a bit like us waiting for someone to take over from me.'

'Is Godot a pianist?' she said.

'No.'

'He's not.'

'Not that I know of.'

It had been always the same with Bryn. All through their touring years he'd prattle away about things quite beyond her or anyone's understanding. Out of nowhere, there he'd be talking rubbish, boring her to death.

'If we knew her number, we could try Jane,' he said.

'No, not Jane!' she retorted.

'She might be free.'

'If you think I'm going to work with Jane you must be mad,' she said. 'My husband Gerald and her in Manchester in that Britannia hotel or whatever it's called – you must be joking,' she said.

'It could just be gossip, you know, about her and Gerald, Gwyneth.'

'The entire membership of the Musicians Union knows what went on with Gerald and that nymphomaniac Jane at the Britannia, Bryn. Don't be so naive,' she cried.

Bryn could be so stupid. She shuddered to think she had actually fancied the moron, just that one time, when they were on tour in Germany, or was it the Isle of Man? She must have been mad. Quite mad. And those cord trousers – didn't he realize how hideous he looked in them?

Sometimes, when things were especially bad, when she wondered what on earth she was doing, travelling here, there and everywhere, she would hark back to all those years earlier when she had trained to be a ballet dancer at Arts Ed. That had been before she was told her feet were too big and her bum too much of a good thing. It had been decided she should concentrate on her singing voice; she had a good voice, everyone said so; and she had gone to the Royal College of Music, the promise of an outstanding career before her. And here she was, stuck in Bristol with a man who gets drunk and breaks his wrist. And there was her mother in Porthcawl, always saying that she ought to have stuck with the ballet, she herself being a tiny woman running dance classes for the under sevens and the over sixties.

'It's by Samuel Becket,' he said, as he checked out contacts on his phone.

'What?'

'The play. Waiting for Godot.'

'Does he ever turn up, this Godot man?'

'No. Not in the play. Actually, in fact, some other men turn up. In the play.'

'Is one of them a pianist?'

Bryn shook his head.

'I still think we ought to try Gerald,' he insisted.

'I am not working with my husband Gerald!' she shouted. 'Oh my God!' she exclaimed, her voice grating, her hand at her throat.

Bryn looked at his watch.

'Amsterdam was the best, don't you think?' she said. 'Of all our overseas dates. The concert hall in Amsterdam.'

'We've not been to Amsterdam,' Bryn said.

'We have been to Amsterdam,' she insisted.

'You've not been with me, not to Amsterdam, Gwyneth.'

'We were in Holland,' she said.

Why couldn't he remember these things? she thought. He was hopeless. He was so unappealing. So colourless. And those trousers, they seemed to look worse on him with every day he wore them.

'It was Rotterdam,' he said.

She couldn't remember Rotterdam.

'Did we like Rotterdam?' she asked.

'No,' Bryn replied.

'We didn't? Where else have we been?' she asked. 'We've been to Denmark. Copenhagen, Odessa. Don't tell me we haven't been to Copenhagen and Odessa.

'Eindhoven. You remember,' he said.

'Eindhoven?'

'Medieval city. After we were in Aarhus and Horsens,' he said. 'Before we went to Bremen. You didn't like Bremen.'

'I didn't like it?' she asked.

'There wasn't much of an audience in Bremen,' he said.

'Do you remember that ghastly Spanish restaurant in Frankfurt? The worst food I've ever tasted,' she said. 'What was it we had?'

'Fish stew.'

'Oh God, it was disgusting. That fish stew, Bryn, it was running with oil, all over the plate. Thick green sticky oil.'

'It was awful,' Bryn said.

'And that terrible man in charge, with the handlebar moustache and the hair coming out of his nose,' she recalled with a pronounced shudder.

'That was in Rotterdam,' Bryn said.

'Frankfurt,' she insisted. 'The Spanish restaurant in Frankfurt.'

'The man with the handlebar moustache, the hair coming out of his nose was at the French restaurant in Rotterdam,' he said. 'The man at the Spanish restaurant in Frankfurt was bald. He was bald. He had a large strawberry mark above his left eye.'

'That was the man in that hotel in Rochdale,' she asserted.

'The man in Rochdale was the man with the hump,' he said. 'That Greek restaurant outside Harrogate – that was where we had that disgusting lasagne which tasted like leather. You remember.'

'That was in Watford,' she said.

'No. In Watford we had the chicken tika which was like leather.'

'Watford was hell,' Gwyneth said.

'That lasagne in Harrogate,' Bryn said with distaste.

'Where?' Gwyneth asked, having lost where they'd got up to.

'Harrogate,' Bryn said.

'Harrogate,' she said.

'That lasagne in Harrogate. It was like leather. Ghastly, Gwyneth.'

'Awful. It was awful, wasn't it?' she said.

'Awful,' he said.

'Quite the most awful Greek restaurant I have ever known,' she said.

'Ghastly,' he said.

'What was?' Gwyneth asked.

'The Greek restaurant outside Harrogate, Gwyneth.'

'Awful,' she said.

'Awful.'

'We've had some marvellous times,' she said.

'Marvellous,' Bryn said.

Gwyneth began to repair her make-up, which was what she did when she was at her wit's end.

'What about that audience in Eastbourne?' she said. 'God help us. Can you believe it? Whistling while I was singing.'

'They recognized the tunes, you see, Gwyneth,' Bryn said.

Bryn's phone rang. He answered it. It was Vic.

'Hello. Vic!' he cried excitedly. 'I've sprained my wrist. Gwyneth and I are in Liverpool tonight. Can you help out?'

'You've got to help us out, Vic!' Gwyneth called.

'Oh, you can't,' Bryn said to Vic.

'You've got to do it, Vic!' Gwyneth shouted.

'Well, never mind. You have a nice time,' Bryn said to Vic.

He rang off.

'He can't do it,' he said to Gwyneth.

'Why, Bryn?! Why can't he do it?!'

'Vic is taking Branwen Roberts to Rome for a few days. It's her birthday. They're flying out tonight.'

'He's going to Rome with Branwen Roberts?!' she yelled. 'With Branwen Roberts the harpist?! Branwen Roberts is my husband Gerald's latest fancy woman. What does she think she's up to going to Rome with Vic? I suppose Gerald's found himself some other bit of skirt, has he? Some flighty trombonist or French horn player. All that blowing and sucking – Gerald goes in for that in a big way – can't resist all that. I'm living on my own from now on,' she said. 'Live on your own. No one to walk in and out on you.'

'Vic says try Barry,' Bryn said.

'Barry?' she said.

'Barry Stevens.'

'Barry's dead.'

'No, he's not.'

'He is. He's dead,' she assured him.

'Where did you hear that?'

'It's common knowledge,' she said. 'I read it in the Musicians Union magazine. In the obituary.'

'Barry Stevens?'

'He's dead,' she said.

'Are you sure?'

'I'm telling you.'

'I can't believe it,' Bryn said. 'Vic said try him, try Barry. You'd think he'd have known if he was dead.'

'Vic's mind is taken up with the Branwen Roberts woman and her harp. He's forgotten.'

'He's forgotten Barry Stevens is dead?'

'Lust can have a most debilitating effect on a man's mental faculties, Bryn. Even you in those unspeakable trousers must know that,' she said.

'I'll phone Barry, just in case though, shall I?' he suggested.

'Oh, my God! Yes, yes, phone him if you have to!' she cried.

Bryn dialled.

It was Barry's voice mail.

'Hello. Barry?' Bryn said. 'It's Bryn Phillips, Barry. Can you phone me back as soon as possible, if you can, old chap? Gwyneth and I are doing a recital in Liverpool tonight, but I've sprained my wrist, fell over, tripped over the hotel carpet. We need a pianist fast and we're wondering if you can help out. If you can't, don't worry.'

'He's dead, for God's sake!' Gwyneth shouted.

'I'm sorry if you're dead, old man,' Bryn said into his phone. 'I'm sorry if this isn't the right time to ask you and all that. Whoever plays back this message, if you're Barry's next of kin or someone, I'm very sorry if I've upset you or anything like that.'

He had run out of things to say, so he rang off.

'Barry's dead,' she said.

She was losing her voice.

'My throat,' she said. 'It's so bloody painful.'

The situation was impossible. Neither of them could think of anything further to say. Gwyneth hated silence. It unnerved her. Bryn knew that. He thought he should say something.

'You remember cigarette cards,' he said. 'I used to collect them. I had thousands. I used to put them in special categories.'

Oh, my God, Gwyneth thought, not this story again.

'I used to collect bottle tops too,' he said. 'Bottle tops and cigarette cards. I started to collect bottle tops and cigarette cards after I was fostered. Used to spend hours with them. It was how I kept out of my foster mother's way. We never really got on, my foster mother and me. I don't know why. She wasn't a very patient woman. Very easily irritated.'

If he went on any more about his foster mother she was going to scream, Gwyneth thought.

'Please God, do something, anything, to make him stop,' Gwyneth muttered.

'She used to say I got under her feet,' he said. 'Used to say I talked too much. Yack, yack, yack, she used to say. What are you yacking on about? she'd say. The only encouraging thing she said to me was when I played the piano. Stop talking and play the piano, she'd say. The last time I saw her – fifteen years ago – in Canada – Toronto – she didn't recognize me. My foster mother said, who are you? And I said, Bryn. And she said, Bryn? And I said, yes. I'm Bryn. I was fostered by you, I lived with you, I said. And she said: what are you yacking on about? And I said: when I was six years old, I came to live with you. You were my foster mother. You took me in. And I learned to play the piano. Her mind had deteriorated, you see. When I said goodbye, after my going over to Canada to see her, she said, who are you? And I said: Bryn. And she said: Bryn? And I said, yes. I'm Bryn. And she said, I've just had one Bryn visiting. And I said, yes, that's me. She didn't recognize me. Only she had become senile. She kept repeating herself. She kept on repeating herself, Gwyneth.'

'I remember you saying, Bryn,' Gwyneth said.

'Her mind had gone. She kept saying the same thing over and over again.'

'There's this big bloke,' Bryn said. 'Pozzo.'

'Phone him. This Pozzo bloke. If he's any good phone him.'

'No, no. He isn't a pianist. Well, he might be, but he's not stated as such in the play, Waiting for Godot. It's just them and a tree. The play. It's sort of about the purposelessness of life. They talk about this and that. Oh, and a boy comes on. With a message from Godot. He's not coming today. In fact, I think he comes on twice, with the same message. In the end they decide to hang themselves. Only they don't. They tried to do so by using the belt of one of them. And –' He was laughing loudly at the thought of it. 'You won't believe it, Gwyneth.'

'His trousers fell down,' she said.

'That's it! His trousers fell down.'

Gwyneth inspected the back of her throat in her hand mirror.

'My throat, it's swollen.'

'I'm phoning Gerald,' Bryn said.

'Oh, my God, no! Not him! No!' Gwyneth said, her hand at her throat, her voice reduced to a strangulated whisper.

'It's Gerald's voice mail,' Bryn said. 'I'll leave a message. Hello, Gerald,' he said into his phone. 'This is Bryn, Gerald.'

Gwyneth rose from her chair, staggered to the bed where she picked up a pillow and hit Bryn about the head with it.

'Gerald, this is Bryn,' he said, trying to ward off Gwyneth's attack. 'I've hurt my hand, Gerald, and I can't play. Gwyneth and I are in Liverpool, tonight. Can you stand in for me? Ring us back, will you? Thanks.'

He rang off.

Gwyneth, energy spent, her throat throbbing, limped back to the chair by the window.

Bryn's phone rang. Bryn answered it.

'Hello. Gerald! It's Gerald!' he said.

'No!' Gwyneth squeaked.

'Gerald, old man. We're in a bit of a hole, Gerald. Gwyneth and me, see. What? Oh. Oh, you can't.'

'Turn the damn thing off. Stop talking to him, for God's sake, Bryn!' Gwyneth squawked.

'Yes, well, it's good to hear you're keeping busy, getting a lot of work, Gerald,' Bryn said. 'And let's hope we see each other again soon.'

Gwyneth lurched across the room, tore the phone from Bryn's hands and threw it across the room.

'What are you doing, Gwyneth?'

'I said don't talk to him!' she yelled.

'He can't do it anyway.'

'Good!' she screeched.

Bryn bent down to pick up the phone. As he began to straighten up his back gave way.

'Oh my God,' he cried out in pain.

He hobbled back to the bed and, holding on with both arms, lowered himself onto it.

'I can't speak,' Gwyneth said.

'I've seized up, Gwyneth. I can't stand up!' Bryn said.

'I can't speak,' she mouthed inaudibly.

'God, my back!' he said.

Bryn's phone rang.

'Hello,' he said into the phone. 'Vic! Vic!' he exclaimed. 'Thanks for getting back to us. You can do it! Oh, good show. You know where? Yes. Right. Thanks, thanks.'

He rang off.

'He's not going to Rome. Branwen Roberts has decided to go back to her husband Derek. We can do the recital, Gwyneth. Vic can play for you! Isn't that great news!'

Gwyneth, exhausted and voiceless, croaked, 'I can't sing, Bryn!'

'Vic can play for you!' he told her.

He was jumping up and down with joy, oblivious to the pain in his back.

'I'm going to kill you. I'm going to kill you!' she rasped. 'And for God's sake, Bryn,' she mouthed, 'ditch that unutterably repulsive green tweed jacket and those appalling blue cord trousers.'

Beyond the window there was lightning and distant thunder.

THE PARK

'The park's alright.'

That's what Pete said when someone asked 'What's the park like, Pete? Working in it?'

'It's alright,' he'd say. 'I'm with Tom's gang. It's me, Tom, Rocky and Andy.'

Pete had done his Level 1 Certificate, Practical Horticulture.

'I done my Level 1,' he'd say.

He was thinking of taking his Level 2. Then, like before, he'd do two mornings a week at college and the rest of the week he'd be in the park. He'd be tidying up, planting out, weeding the flower beds, dead heading the rose garden. That was what Pete did.

It'd been raining all that summer, the rain flattening everything. They'd been out all morning securing and staking up damaged shrubs and plants and removing broken branches.

It was coming up to two o'clock. It was overcast, south west winds threatening more rain.

Pete and Tom were standing by the tarpaulins that covered the ground in front of the recently erected fountain where they were to lay turf for the following day's ceremony. They folded the tarpaulins and hauled them over to the nearby rhododendrons. Tom was the foreman. He'd been working the parks for twenty years. He was a man of few words. Lived with his wife in Streatham.

Rocky, in his regulation yellow donkey-jacket, wheeled in the topsoil from the truck he'd parked on the path leading off the Main Walk.

Early that morning he'd been on the tractor cutting the grass. It was waterlogged, he had said to Ron Derridge in the park office. Ron Derridge reminded him that there was to be the unveiling ceremony of the Lord Keddick fountain the next day. The fountain had been erected in memory of the late Lord Keddick who had been largely responsible for financing the building of the new concert hall. The mayor, government and park officials and Lord Keddick's widow would be attending. Rocky was directed to mow the grass as best he could.

'And now it looks an effing mess,' Rocky said to Tom and Pete.

Andy – 'Marxist' Andy, as Rocky called him – wheeled in spades and rakes. He was in his fifties, same as Tom. He reckoned Lord Keddick, being a multi-millionaire, what he had paid out would have been little more to him than chicken feed.

Rocky dumped the top soil over the ground that they had dug over and covered with the tarpaulins the day before. Pete and Andy raked it. Tom raked in the fertilizer.

'It's sodden,' Rocky said.

'We ought to leave it for two or three days to settle, Tom,' Pete said.

'There you have it, Tom,' Rocky said. 'Pete, the high-flying apprentice, he's the expert.'

'I'm not an apprentice, Rocky. I'm a full-time employee, aren't I, Tom?' Pete said.

'My God,' Rocky said. 'There's no need to make a song and dance about it, is there, boy?'

Calling him 'boy' was like bullying. Like his mum said. Like when he was at school. He wasn't to let anyone push him around, that's what his dad who was in advertising said.

They heeled in the top soil. They walked it all over, pressing down on their heels, removing stones and clumps of earth.

'I'm a dad,' Pete said. 'Me and Cath got a baby boy. Baby Max. I'm not no 'boy'. I'm a dad, aren't I?'

'You seen your kid?' Andy said.

'Yeah. 'Course.'

'I mean recent?'

'No, no – Cath's not well, is she?' Pete said.

She was depressed. It was biological. It happened to some women when they'd given birth, his dad had told him. When she was better, he'd be able to see her and the baby again.

They got the turf from off the back of the truck.

They rolled it out.

After a while they could hear music coming from the Open-Air Theatre in the park.

'Matinee performance,' Rocky said.

'The play's started, Tom,' Pete said. 'Midsummer Night's Dream.'

'Now, fair Hippolyta, our nuptial hour draws on apace,' Rocky said.

'Rocky knows the words,' Pete said.

'That's Theseus speaking, it is,' Rocky said. 'Then he's off backstage for a fag and a quick grope of the leading lady.'

It was always the same. It was Midsummer Night's Dream almost every summer. Rocky said it was the same thing every time.

'The great and good,' Rocky said, 'will be going to that play after tomorrow's commemoration.'

'You wait till you see what they're going to charge for tickets to go to that concert hall of theirs,' Andy said.

They were laying the turf, butt-jointing the ends tightly so as to knit the turf together.

They spaded up the top soil, added sand and soil into gaps.

It was work that couldn't be rushed.

'Time for a short break,' Tom said.

Rocky went for a slash, for teas from the park café for him and Andy.

Pete had his sandwich, his bottle of cola. He had to eat, he said. He'd had his lunch. His mum made it. This is a bit extra, she'd said. He'd got to put on weight. She'd said that all the time, he'd got to eat, the physical work he did. She'd knocked up sandwiches that morning before he left home, and he took the Tube from Highgate. Ham, cheese, tomatoes – he didn't like tomato – lettuce, brown bread, a bottle of apple juice. The apple juice was good for him, she'd said. Vitamin C.

He got out his iPhone. Someone nicked his old one. His mum and dad bought him the one he had now, told him to look after it. It'd got the lot; internet, Instagram, Facetime, music, games, camera.

Tom sat himself on the lower ledge of the fountain. His back was playing up.

He'd got a boat, up at Winkwell Dock. Grand Union Canal. Viking 23. Bought it second hand. It was called Betsy Wilton. It'd been called that when he'd bought it. Weekends, he and his wife and sister and her husband took the boat out on the Grand Union Canal – Berkhamstead, Hemel Hempstead, Watford. They'd stop off at The Three Horseshoes for something to eat. They took the boat, maximum speed four miles an hour, through Berkhamsted,

Tring, and on through Kings Langley. From the Tring Summit they'd go into the Chilterns. Beautiful countryside. On his holiday the previous year, he and his wife had taken it towards Rugby.

His wife, Sheila, had said he ought to retire. That back of his was only going to get worse. She said he could help out a few days a week at her brother's butcher's in Elford Street.

Rocky came back with mugs of tea for him and Andy.

'I've been assaulted by that fecking Alsatian – that fella with the Alsatian. Kick its fecking teeth in I will one of these days,' he said. 'That Alsatian, Tom. On one of them leads what goes on for miles. Come back, the stupid sod is calling and the fecking animal is halfway to the White Cliffs of Dover. Them old women, they're out there again this afternoon – dancing in a circle. What I think is, they're casting a spell on us all, dancing around like the three fecking witches. Fecking amazing. That man is there, seated himself, he is, on a bench, Pete, waiting for you, he is. You'd not want to disappoint the man. He's got his sweetie bag out, he has.'

'I don't go near him,' Pete said.

Rocky and Andy drank their tea. Tom had a bottle of water, Pete his sandwich and cola.

Pete stuck earphones in and played music on his iPhone.

'It's Eminem. Rocky, Eminem,' he said.

They could hear music and actors' indistinct voices carried on the southwest wind from the Open-Air Theatre.

'That's Demetrius and his bird in the woods,' Rocky said. 'The poor fecking girl, she's desperate she is. That Demetrius actor, he's got some lungs on him.'

Andy lit a cigarette. He got a text from his wife. Their older boy had had a fall at school, had done something to his ankle.

'She'd gone to collect him,' he said. 'She's having to leave the young one with her mother round the corner.'

Her boss at the solicitors where she worked in reception was okay when she had to take time off because of the kids, he said.

Pete was cleaning the muck out of the fountain and spading it into a wheelbarrow, while the others carried on laying the turf.

Ron Derridge from the park office turned up.

'You mother's in the office, Pete' he said. 'She's come to see you.'

He didn't want her coming. Her making a fuss. Like he was stupid. He didn't want her coming to see how he was getting on. He'd told her before.

'We're laying the turf,' Pete said. 'We got a job to do.'

Pete was best left alone to work things out for himself, that was what Andy, Rocky and Tom had come to learn. Pete worked, did his bit. One could do a lot worse, Tom had said.

They were rolling the turf, cutting, spading, and levelling. Only the wind picking up in the tree tops and a plane overheard could be heard. And the occasional words and snatches of music from the Open-Air Theatre. A dog barking. The shouts of children playing. The squeaky tuneless song of a lone dunnock scratching about in the undergrowth. The tapping of spade on turf. Tom's breathing. His wife, Sheila, had spoken about his breathing.

'Hey! I've got photos,' Pete said. 'It's Ben. On Facebook My Cath, and Ben and Jake is outside Sunny's, larking about. Jake and Cath doing a dance. Hey! She get better and then off we go, eh? Her and me and the kid. Eh, Tom? Hey! Picture here. Jake's bike – motorbike. His Yamaha YBR 125 – I been on it!'

'You're doing out that fountain good, Pete,' Andy said.

'I'm doing it good, Tom,' Pete said.

'Keeping working at it,' Tom said.

'You got him joining your Workers Revolutionary Party, Andy, have you?' Rocky said.

'You want to try thinking before you come out with all that crap.' Andy said.

'You take my advice, Pete, you'll not get yourself caught up in all that Union malarkey,' Rocky said. 'Now me, live and let live, that's my motto. Wine, women and song, Pete. You want to come out Friday, Saturday night, a few beers.'

Friday, Saturday nights Rocky could be found strutting his stuff at the Red Brick Planet Club. He'd be done up in his button-down shirt, dark jeans, Ralph Lauren black leather shoes. He'd been kicked out of the last place where he was living, him coming back at three in the morning, drunk, and making a dickhead of himself. He was now having to make do with a sofa at a mate's place in Paddington.

'The women in the Red Brick Planet Club, some cracking good-looking women come in there, mate,' he said. 'Gasping for it, they are. You want to forget Andy and his union bollocks.'

'Fancy yourself, don't you, Rocky, eh?' Andy said. 'In your 40's, behaving like you're one of the kids.'

'Eff off,' Rocky said. 'Bugger off to Russia with the rest of your comrades!'

'Oy! The two of you. Give over!' Tom shouted.

'That's it. All done,' Tom said.

He took a board, laid it across one corner of the turf, trod on it lightly so as to ensure contact between the soil and the underside of the turf. It was half past four.

Andy lit a cigarette.

'The fountain's cleaned out,' Pete said.

They started to gather up the tools.

'Thus die I, thus, thus, thus,' Rocky declaimed. 'Now am I dead, Now am I fled.'

'Rocky knows it – the play,' Pete said.

'That's Pyramus speaking. Matinee's nearly done,' Rocky said.

Ron Derridge came over from the park office.

'It's done, Ron,' Pete said to him.

Ron looked it over.

'I've just heard: Len's dead,' he said.

'Old Len. He worked here a good long time, he did,' Rocky said. 'Worked down at the lakeside.'

'He was a one-off,' Andy said. 'He had his lunch break on his own, his sandwich, his apple, his bottle of water, in the shed down there where they've built the concert hall. That was Len's shed.'

'That was him,' Tom said.

'He knew the park like the back of his hand,' Rocky said.

'Good job, eh, Ron?' Pete said, referring to the turf.

'Yep,' Ron said.

'It's a good job, Tom,' Pete said.

'After the ceremony tomorrow, all this has to come up and paving put down,' Ron said. 'Cos of health and safety, kids playing with the water, one of them might slip, fall and hurt themselves. Sorry about that. Lord Keddick's widow has made it known the fountain dedicated to her husband's memory is to be fronted by grass. Apparently, her husband loved lawns. After the ceremony, it's paving stones.'

Tom picked up a flat board to clean it off.

'Well, there we are then,' Rocky said. 'Fecking Health and Safety.'

'As I say, word has come down from senior management,' Ron said.

'We put down that turf and now it's going to be paving stones. Might as well chuck it all in,' Tom said.

'It's out of my hands,' Ron said.

They could hear the sound of trumpets and applause coming from the Open-Air Theatre.

'Get the wheelbarrow and rakes together,' Tom said to Pete.

Swifts on the wing were soaring high and wheeling over the trees, calling to each other with high-pitched screams.

'It's driving I want – drive the tractors like Rocky, Ron,' Pete said. 'I'm going to take driving lessons, aren't I, Tom?'

'God help us, you're not driving my fecking tractor, Pete,' Rocky said.

Andy got a text from his wife. She was taking the boy to A&E. The younger one was with his nan, he said.

Ron Derridge went back to the office.

Tom and Pete wheeled the tools to the truck.

Andy and Rocky, lifted the tarpaulins by the rhododendrons and followed them.

'It looks good, Tom,' Pete said.

*

The night before the ceremony was to take place, vandals evaded the security officers and sprayed the fountain with white paint. The ceremony was postponed. Andy, Tom, Rocky and Pete were questioned by the police. Andy's house and garden were searched.

None of them were charged. Another contractor oversaw the removal of the turf and laying of paving stones.

That Autumn Tom took early retirement, did gardening jobs for people living around where he lived in Streatham.

The park management reduced the workforce. Rocky went to Spain to help out a mate run his bar. Andy and Pete stayed on at the park working with different teams. Pete's Cath told him he wasn't the boy's dad. His dad was someone else. She didn't know who the father was, she said.

'What's the park like, Pete? Working in it?' someone would say.

'It's alright,' he'd say.

JACK

This is a story about a man called Jack.

It was very important to Jack to keep busy. Not to do so left him feeling unduly empty. Who was he, when not fully occupied? It was a question he declined to address. A question he sidestepped, had no time to consider. That was Jack. Make no mistake, he was valued. He had his worth; his job at Central Industries. He'd won a prize, a commendation, best management administration award 2016. Not bad. Very good. Only, once received, he found he felt compelled to be even more busy than when he had been at his busiest. That was Jack. It was when he got home to his house in Ladbroke Grove, he felt the emptiness. So, he didn't go home, not until much later than his work required of him. He would stay on at his office that was on the third floor until after ten, then go home, and, exhausted, fall into bed. That was Jack.

It came about that one evening Jack discovered that in an office down on the second floor, seated at a desk in export-import, was a man he'd not ever seen before. A man called Martin. Martin confessed that he hadn't been home for over six months, hadn't left the office in all that time, except for lunch, a take-away from the nearby deli. He hadn't been home, he admitted, because he hadn't a home. He'd lost his home to his wife after he and she had divorced.

So, he had stayed at work, as in his own way and in accordance with his own needs, Jack had done.

Jack was much touched by Martin's story, his circumstances. And without much thought on the matter, in fact no thought at all, for thought would cause hesitation, Jack leapt to the call. He took up Martin's cause. He invited him to come to live with him. That was best, Jack said, and Martin, being a man who gave in readily to other's expectations, agreed; he moved in with Jack, and Jack was pleased. Here, after all, was something in life to occupy Jack other than work, other than the Company.

Things quietened down after that. Both men busied themselves with making a home for the two of them. Martin's room had to be decorated and furnished, a bed selected and purchased, a side table, lamp, shelves, chest of drawers. The living room which they now shared had to be rearranged, another lamp over a second armchair, a new carpet to give the room a freshness, a sense of purpose. They were both leaving work early, on the dot of 5.30. No one seemed to notice. Days were taken off so that they could visit Ikea, Habitat, the John Lewis lighting department. They preferred not to shop online as it was best, they said, that they viewed potential purchases in person, tried them out, discussed the pros and cons with the sales staff and between themselves. Jack was the forerunner, the leader. Martin was happy to be 'second banana', as he liked to say of himself, to be in a supporting role. That's how they were. And that worked well. Until Marje came on the scene. Big, boisterous, cheery, sweep-all-in-front-of- her, Marje. Not a bad looker. Martin had met Marje at the cheese counter in Waitrose. He had been thinking of buying Roquefort. But Marje had appeared at his side and had recommended and persuaded him to buy mozzarella.

Marje had a liking for passive men. So, Martin was the man for her; well, for the time being. Martin was pliant, a bit of a pushover, and that was what Marje valued in a male. It suited her. Not for her the Jacks of this world. Not pushy self-confident types like Jack; such were altogether too much trouble. She had tried a 'Jack' once, and it had been a disaster, led to conflict, even to shouting. The man in question, a fellow called Peter, finished up, before she finished with him, with a black eye.

In Martin's eyes, Marje was well-rounded, she was generously bosomed. In the manner in which she confronted and negotiated the world, she was to him a sort of female Jack. A 'Jack Plus'. He lay in his recently purchased John Lewis bed in his recently allotted bedroom, the walls of which had been painted in Farrow and Ball elephant grey emulsion, and anticipated voluptuous out-size Marje at his side, naked, the two of them having engaged in the most satisfying sex, in much better sex than he had experienced with his ex-wife, whose name was Carol, he remembered, a name which was not at all as attractive as the name Marje, he told himself.

As for Jack, he was appalled by the change in Martin, and by the arrival on the scene of Marje whom he didn't take to at all. Far, far too bossy; quite clearly intent on taking over, being the centre of attention, having her way all the time and in all things. He warned Martin against her. But Martin smiled limply and shrugged, and one Saturday morning Jack rose to discover Marje in the kitchen making Martin's breakfast; egg, bacon, Heinz baked beans, toast, Wilkins' chunky marmalade; she was wearing Martin's purple and yellow polka dot dressing gown and, it was beyond doubt, she had shared Martin's bed that night.

'I can't have this,' Jack said to Martin.

The only thing Martin could expect to do was move out and move in with Marje, but the thought of that left Jack feeling redundant. And anyway, it transpired, Marje's flat was just too small. It was hardly big enough for her alone. Of course, Marje could possibly move in with Martin and Jack. Jack didn't know who suggested this. But it happened. There was Marje the following day arriving in a taxi with several suitcases and other bits and pieces. Martin's room was too small for both him and Marje, whereas Jack's room was nearly twice the size, so, Jack didn't know who suggested it and how it came about, but Marje, along with her belongings and with Martin, moved into Jack's room and Jack moved into Martin's.

Marje didn't like the new carpet, so it was agreed they bought a brighter one which Jack hated but he wasn't saying. He was thinking, not something he was accustomed to be doing, but he had no alternative. He was working out how to regain his ascendancy.

Then Carol, Martin's ex-wife, turned up, a skinny woman who had had a bit of a breakdown as a consequence of her break-up with Martin, and as she sat in their living room, looking tearful, Jack felt he had discovered the answer to his problems, to his feeling of being at a loose end, of having time on his hands, of not being sufficiently occupied. That was to say, he took a liking, was attracted to her evident dependency upon others. He 'made a move on her', as the saying had it. He tried to help her feel less, a little less, not too much less, but enough less vulnerable so as to attract her to him, to look to him for support, for understanding of her circumstances.

And all was going well, until one day, not so long after Carol arrived on the scene, she and Martin announced they were getting back together again. How this had come about Jack couldn't say. He hadn't a clue. One minute, Carol was all over Jack, and then there she was, telling him she was going back to Martin, that they were intending to remarry, for God's sake. Their few years of marriage, those times they had shared were too precious for them to be discarded, thrown away as if they had never been, he was told. The following day Martin and Carol left. And there was Jack and Marje. Two bulls in the proverbial china shop.

Then there was Peter. Who was Peter? Jack had to ask himself. Then he remembered. Peter was Marje's ex, to whom, before she had walked out, she had given a black eye.

Peter turned up out of the blue. A weak jelly fish of a man, as Jack perceived him to be. Jack had come back from Sainsbury's, and there in the living room was Marje and Peter. And Marje, at that time having no one to dominate, had found herself in a quandary; so, there was Peter, and Marje decided that for the time being at least, she would reunite with Peter and in doing so would thereby rediscover her self-worth and proper place in the world.

After they left, Jack looked about the flat that no longer felt like his own, and decided to return to the office where, he became aware, he had been working less and less. He took his place at his desk and stayed until after ten at night, on one occasion visiting the floor below to ascertain whether or not Martin or someone else might be there, someone like himself who couldn't face being at home with time on their hands, but there was no one. Seated at his desk, which he had for so long mostly neglected, he saw a note, a note he didn't remember having seen before, on the computer screen, a note, dated the first of the month, from the departmental manager informing him that his services were no longer required, that from the end of the current month he should consider himself no longer in the Company's employ.

There is no end to this story. No resolution. How could there be?

After Carol had again left Martin, and Marje had left Peter, with Marje marrying a Canadian owner of an 'ass-paper' mill, and Carol meeting and co-habiting with a grocer called Evans, Peter heard that Martin – was his name Martin? – had returned to Jack, and Jack and he resolved to start over again. Both men busied themselves with making a home for the two of them. Martin's room had to be redecorated. And once more everything became fine and dandy. Then the day came when Julia, jolly, argumentative, judo black belt Julia came on the scene, and made a move on Martin, and Martin…

THAT'S ALL RIGHT, SHE SAYS

He saw a young girl die today. Not a young girl, she was twenty-four. Not his child, yet for eleven years in his care. It was her leg that did it. Finally. Her leg, he said to her mother, had to come off. It might save her. Or it might not. Her mother knew. They were outside the girl's hospital room. Her mother nodded, tears in her eyes, tears again welling.

They had the leg off on the Monday morning. The girl had consented. She was dead by the following afternoon.

She used to say from time to time, 'How are the boys?' 'The older one, her age, is up at Bristol University now,' he'd said to her. She'd asked about him before: 'He's in his school first eleven, cricket,' he'd said. 'He's taking his A levels, Physics, Maths, Politics. The younger one –' 'Yes, how is the younger one, how is Tim?' she'd asked. 'Tim's a slow learner. Good lad, but no academic. Tim's in the school play. Enjoys the drama,' he told her. He had said this about Tim and the drama with a downturn of the mouth. 'So long as he's happy,' she'd said to him.

'I think we're going to have to amputate the leg,' he says to her. 'That's all right,' she says.

Christ. Christ above, he'd known her all this time as the girl, his girl, thirteen years old. 'It's rheumatoid arthritis, a chronic progressive disease,' he told her mother. Inflammation of the joints. Painful deformity, loss of function, effecting lungs, heart, kidneys. How was he to explain, how to avoid medical jargon? Her body had turned against her, was at war with her. Twenty-four years of age now. Twenty-four, and she says, 'That's all right.'

Poor consultant Dr Rintaul, she's thinking. He doesn't know, but she heard him with his acolytes and her mother outside in the corridor by her open door. 'It's the leg or she's got two weeks,' she heard him confide. Off they went.

The man's looking older. She'll not tell him. His hair is much greyer. The lines down the side of his nose are more pronounced. Poor Mrs Rintaul, his wife at home in Beaconsfield, what she has to put up with, with a man like him with his bravado, his coming home in the evening, this dark bear, this bluff giant at her dinner table.

Who'd be in his shoes? Not I, she thinks. Not this young woman, his patient since she was only thirteen years old. How long ago would that be? Her brain is going down the drain, she says to herself. She has a university degree, a Master of Arts, studied for it in her flat; the tutor, students visiting, setting up class in her small living room. But her brain is treading the primrose path. 'It deteriorates, as if by the day,' she says to herself.

Claude Monet's 'The Bridge at Argenteuil' is on the wall of her hospital room. Her mother had it put there.

She turns her head on the raised pillows towards the window. Nice day out there. Sunny. A white cloud is moving into view.

Thirteen she was when it came on, took its hold, that day, standing at the railway station, seeing her father off for the last time, looking up at him standing at the carriage window, and she discovered she couldn't move her legs. Growing pains, the doctor said. She'll get over it. Thirteen years of age. Eleven years ago.

Poor Alec Rintaul, she thinks. He hadn't a grey hair on his head, not then. She's worn out the poor man. He has been fighting a losing battle. First the knees. The hands, the fingers. The joints locked, twisted, the muscle wasted. The tests, the drugs, the operations, the knees, the hips, then the spleen.

Dr Rintaul. All cross and in a rush he comes. Knowing what he knows, he can hardly look her in the face. He towers above her bed with its special mattress that keeps her bones from bruising. He turns to his team. His patient looks on. She observes. She has dissociated herself. It is her way now.

The great man is addressing her. She observes he is flustered. His junior doctor appears exhausted. His registrar waits on him. She is pale.

'You have a choice,' he is saying.

He rattles off the names of new drugs. Credibility has languished, has become a scarecrow. That is your choice, he is saying, the drugs are nasty. There is no guarantee.

He turns away. He is heading for the door. He turns again to his patient. The dark shadow of his jaw and jowls reddens. Why did he choose such a career? He is speaking. She makes an effort to hear his words.

'Dr Ruskin here,' he says of his young registrar, 'will answer your questions.'

Dr Ruskin, a woman in her thirties, quite pretty, brown hair to her shoulders. She nods in the patient's direction.

'Yes, of course. I'll pop by in half an hour,' she says. They go.

All those years ago, when she and Dr Rintaul first met, when at the age of thirteen, she stood before him in her vest and knickers, her cheeks burning. This man had been in his early forties then, a bachelor. Had used to play rugby union for the Harlequin Wanderers. Too old for that now, he had told her, had spoken thus so as to make her comfortable, to distract her. When she first met him, he had just taken up golf. He told the girl he was getting married. He has two boys now. The school fees go up every year. One of the boys, whose name is Peter, plays rugby union, as opposed to rugby league, he has told her. He knew she'd be interested. Peter is athletic. Mr Rintaul is proud of him. She likes the sound of the young one, Tim.

'Is your son – Peter – still playing rugby union?' she asked him today.

He comes in the following week, he and his courtiers. There are students too, who do not like to seem to stare, who look here and there, in this place and that about the room. She does not wish to embarrass them by appearing to examine them too closely. Dr Rintaul tries a smile.

'You've taken a turn for the better,' she hears him say. 'How are you feeling today?' he says. He doesn't expect a reply.

'Did your son – Peter – did his team win on Saturday?' she asks.

'Oh, yes,' he cheerfully replies.

'My boy,' he explains to the students. 'In his school rugger team. Beat the First Fifteen Reserve team seventeen points to three.'

The students pretend interest.

'I'll come and see you this afternoon,' she hears him say. That's ominous, she thinks. He is out there in the corridor.

He says to her mother: 'The only thing we can do is amputate. Remove her leg from above the knee.' Who will break the news?

Poor Dr Rintaul, she thinks. Dear sweet Jesus, let him have a pleasant weekend. Let him win at golf. Let him have his favourite dinner, a couple of pints before Sunday dinner at his local. Dear God, let the thriller he's bought from WH Smith's be a good gripping yarn. He so likes a thriller. Loves John le Carré. Graham Greene. Reads Ken Follett and Wilbur Smith. Dear Jesus, let him come back refreshed and self-confident, for on Monday morning, ever so early, he will stand before her unconsciousness, a General at the Front, holding out against overwhelming odds.

He's at the golf club, on the 13th hole with his golfing chum, Bernie. It's his turn. Only for the moment he can't rise to the occasion, do what's necessary, get on with it.

Bernie says, 'All right?'

'Yes,' he says, and swings his club.

That evening at the restaurant, it's his older boy Peter's birthday.

'You're a bit quiet,' his wife says to him.

'Sorry,' he says.

'He's tired,' she says to everyone.

'Works too hard,' Peter says.

They've been discussing selling up their holiday home in Portugal. The boys are grown up, they want to make their own holiday arrangements. It'd be nice for the mother and father to make a change, be more adventurous, travel to other Countries. Italy. Morocco. Turkey.

'I fancy going back to that Greek Island, Santorini,' he said.

'Spain,' his wife said. 'Seville, Granada.'

That evening, in bed, his wife with a book, he says, 'I saw a young girl die today.'

His wife puts her book down.

'Oh dear, I'm sorry,'

There's nothing more to say. He will speak more about it, if he wants to.

After a moment or two, she returns to her book.

CARRIE'S STORY

Here's a picture of Sammy, three months old. Here's one of me and John outside the hospital. There's Moira. Along with the others, women and kids, with their banners, 'I am Sammy'. There's me and John holding hands, and the cameras, the press, Pro-Life from the USA. And Italy. John met the Pope. They flew him over. Met him in the Vatican. The Pope said to him, he wished us every success and the Catholic Church were praying for us and for the baby. An ambulance was waiting around the corner of the hospital, waiting to take us and Sammy to the airport, to fly us to the doctors in the USA. John was so brave then. He stood up in court and shouted 'You're murdering our baby'. It was in the papers, on the front page. 'Murdered,' it said.

When they turned off his life support, he didn't die. Not straight away. He could have lived, that's what John said to the papers. What he shouted.

After Sammy were gone, it was just me and John. We'd had the life taken out of us. That's how it felt. Him and me in the house, John back at work, people not wanting to say anything. We got a nice letter from Pro-Life in the States, but then it was just me and John. And no Sammy. No fight on our hands no more. John, as I say, back at work, at his office for the Water Company. I wasn't up to going back to work. I had to rest, that's what John said, that's what the doctor said. He said I were understandably depressed, worn out. He said, I needed to take my time.

Moira arrived out of the blue. On the anniversary of Sammy's fifth birthday. She'd found us, she said. She'd seen John getting on a train after work, coming home from work, and she'd followed him. She'd found the courage, she said, to ring the doorbell.

It was Sammy's fifth, and me and John agreed we'd not overdo it. It was time to move on. He said we ought to not have the cake or the candles. He wanted me to go out, go to the pictures. Distract myself, that's what he was saying. He went off to work, and she was at the door. Moira. Freezing to death out there, she said. It'd been snowing for over a week. The coldest November in quite some years, the papers said. She was there and I couldn't say no, sorry, could I, couldn't say, sorry, me and John have decided to put it behind us. She was there, and I recognized her. It was Moira what gave me and John a hug, who was out there shouting with everyone. She was so excited to see me, and she were wearing my dress, the white floral dress. She'd got on the same dress what I'd worn outside the High Court that last day. The dress what I kept all them years in the wardrobe upstairs, what I'd been wearing on the anniversaries of Sammy's birthdays. What me and John decided I'd not wear that time on Sammy's fifth.

Moira said I ought to wear the dress, and I went upstairs and changed, came down into the front room and the both of us were wearing the same dress. She'd made hers herself, she said. And loads of people like her had done the same. And they wore it on the anniversaries of Sammy's birthdays. It was so exciting. She showed me all the photos she had on her iPad; Sammy in his baby-grow, me, John, the banners, pictures of Pro-Life groups in the States.

We set up a shrine in the front room on the sideboard; Sammy's photos, his teddy, photos outside the Court, the hospital, his little white socks, the bunny rabbit all-in-one body suit. I brought out the cake I'd baked. I'd baked the cake, without John knowing. I thought I'd bake it, like before, just in case, so I could have a piece when he was at the office, if I needed. Me and Moira put the candles on, five candles and I lit them and I opened a bottle of red wine, and we toasted his memory, like me and John had done before. Me and Moira, with Sammy's shrine, the cake and the bottle of wine. And we both had a cry.

Then John came home. I say to him, 'Oh, look, who's here? It's Moira,' I say to him, and he looks all straightlaced. Him in his dark grey office suit and his briefcase. He didn't want me to celebrate Sammy's birthday, that's what the look on his face were saying. He didn't make any sort of welcome to Moira. He tried to stop me inviting her for dinner. The dinner was in the oven, chicken like John liked it. And he says no, she can't stay, but I'm not having that. I tell him, she's staying.

Moira said she had to clean up, went to the bathroom upstairs. We'd both looked a bit of a mess, what with the cake and wine. While she was up there, John made known his displeasure. We were making strides and she comes along and puts us back to square one, he said. She was using us. Using us for her own purposes. I told him it was what she believes in. She has a right to her beliefs. She thinks ending a child's life is against God's law. He said she had no right to impose her beliefs on others. I told him, I said, that's all very well, John, but we believed, didn't we? We believed in Sammy's right to live. Sammy could have been saved, that were what it was about. That were what John himself had said. The doctors in the USA said they had a new treatment; Sammy would have had a chance. We believed, didn't we? I said to him. Him having a go at Moira, her coming here, her fighting for her beliefs, he seemed to forget what we was fighting for. We're not Christians, he said. Not in the way she is. We got married in church, but that were it. It doesn't mean we're Christians, he said, it don't mean we have to sign up as full-time members of the Pro-Life lobby. I said to him we did, we signed up when it came to Sammy. There was no arguing with that. I told him. I was shouting.

When she came down, Moira said she had to go, she had to meet someone, she said. She was embarrassed. I told John he'd ruined everything, ruined Sammy's birthday anniversary. If he didn't want Moira to stay for dinner, he could eat his on his own. I wasn't hungry. I went to bed. When he came up later, as far as he were concerned, I was asleep. He'd tidied up downstairs, tidied it all away, the cake, the wine, the shrine me and Moira put up. We didn't speak about it after that. It was better that way.

John and me moved house. It was his idea. It was a nice house. It wasn't very different from our old house. A bit bigger. And our old furniture fitted in. John got a new job. I was doing three mornings a week at Argos. And then after we was living there two years, we had a baby. A baby boy and John were so excited, he was over the moon, we both was. A brand-new baby. We couldn't think of a name for him, we went through all the names. We decided on one or two, then changed our minds. Peter, Larry. Then it was Martin and Richard. We thought Colin would be good. Or Terence. Every day, after John came back from work, and at the weekends, we'd go through the names. We'd take turns wheeling our baby in his carrycot in the front room. John was there, taking him on a world tour round the front room, he said. Then baby became Morris which were the name of an uncle of mine and of a friend John knew at school, and John opened a bottle and we toasted him. Morris. He'll play for Arsenal, John kept saying.

Moira turned up one Friday evening after John came back from work. She'd read about the baby. It was in all the papers and on social media, she said. She was covered in snow from top to bottom. She'd read about the baby and she had come to see him. She was so happy for us. She kept on saying his name, over and over. I got her to hold him. But she wasn't used to it. Afraid she was going to drop him. She'd got it on her iPad, the pictures of the baby, in the papers, everywhere – all over. 'Carrie and John Botham's baby'. 'The happy couple.' 'Happy at Last'. 'Sammy's mum and dad happy at last'. There was a bit from the Pro-Life Movement in the USA – 'God bless dear Carrie and John Botham and their new born baby. God has heard their prayers, has held them dear and blessed them'. Pennsylvania Pro-Life said it were wonderful news, we had been rewarded from above for our bravery and determination'. Moira said as how Baby Morris were a star. She wanted us to go to a meeting in the Community Centre. A public discussion, she said. A Pro-Life debate. One of the Pro-Life people, someone important, a woman Moira knew, were the Chair, and someone from Pro-Choice were the guest speaker, and she wanted us to go with her, make ourselves known, Carrie and John Botham, Sammy's mum and dad. It were over five years ago, but me and John was heroes, she said. We were celebrated as important fixtures in the struggle. Only, for a while after Morris were born, I hadn't been myself. I'd wander about the house, I'd go out, to the shops, the park. I didn't know what I was doing, who I was. And John was at work all day. I said to her I was sorry, I wasn't up to it, I weren't ready.

John kept asking her questions, like he was interviewing her – where she live? Her education. Her mum and dad. She hadn't got a dad, she said. He went off when she was little. There were just her and her mum, her mum in Eastbourne who she visited now and then. Has she a boyfriend? he says. Why not? he says. Didn't she like men? he say to her. I try and stop him. I say, Give over, John. You've not got no right to go prying into her life like this. Her relationship with men is her own business, I tell him. It makes no difference. When John is on a run, he's on it, he's like a bulldog, he won't let go. What's wrong with asking her questions? he's saying.

Then he says all right, he's going to the meeting, he's changed his mind. He wants to find out what all the fuss is about.

I'd gone to bed by the time he got back. He got back in, it was eleven o'clock and he were banging about the house, the bedroom, going on about the meeting, saying as how Moira's lot, as he called them, was hurling abuse at the guest speaker, not letting him get a word out, shouting him down, and when John stood up and suggested they hear him out they started on him, he said, start calling him out, having a go at him, he said. Fuck Moira and all of them, they're a load of fascists, he shouts.

Of course, he'd gone to the pub after. He was always going to the pub them days, he'd be there most nights after work. He said as how he'd felt left out. With it being just me and the baby, he says. He was better off in the pub, why bother to come home? He could go there and have a drink with ordinary people, talk about football, West Ham, Man United. Just chat, no pressure, just be with ordinary men and women, he said. I told him, you have a baby, all those months, nine months, it is natural, the baby need his mum.

The dress what I wore outside the High Court, and on Sammy's birthdays, I wore that dress in Callucio's. When he would have been four. I wore it in memory of him. In memory. I went out in it one afternoon, lunchtime – went to the restaurant Callucio's in the High Street, by myself. Had a meal in Callucio's. Me and the dress. I was sort of afraid someone would notice – recognize me with the dress. I didn't think I'd know what to say or how they'd take it with me wearing it.

I've not got it now, the dress with the flower pattern, the one Moira and all of them copied. I took it to the Oxfam shop. I go back a week later it's hanging there in the window. About two weeks later it wasn't there anymore. Someone bought it. Someone else, somewhere, were wearing it.

Moira turned up again. It must have been a couple months or so since John went to that meeting of hers. She wanted us to join a protest about a baby in another hospital where they wanted to remove his life support. And she wanted me and John to be interviewed by the people on the television, make ourselves known for the cause. Only, John says no. We weren't going. It'd make me ill again. She and John come to words. Start shouting. She called us traitors, blames John, tells me I ought to leave him. The two of them shouting, and John makes to hit her. He tells her to get out, opens the door, tells her to fuck off.

After she'd gone, there was me and him and the baby. And the baby crying because of it all. I said to him he'd hit her. He said he didn't. But if I hadn't shouted at him to stop, he would have. You hit her, I said. Hit, hit, hit. Hit.

Sammy wasn't the one to give up. He'd have gone on if he could. He could have. It's like he's there, up there, he's speaking, saying to me he could have. We ought to have stuck together after everything. Only after Sammy was gone I had a breakdown, and John went off with that woman for five weeks. Sammy only gone six months. He didn't want to talk about it. He said he needed a break.

We was having this blazing row. I shout at him as how he gave up on Sammy. He told the doctor at the hospital he'd try to persuade me to let the hospital switch off his life support. John says it weren't like that. It were the doctor who suggested he talk to me about it. Only, I tell him, I tell him he hadn't told the doctor that we was fighting on, had he? He hadn't said that we were NOT giving up, had he?!

That kid in the hospital Moira was telling us about, the doctors said he couldn't be saved. Only his mum and dad don't want to believe it. They want the right thing for their baby, they were putting up a fight, like what we did.

John said he wanted to go to the protest at the hospital, like Moira wanted. He'd changed his mind. He wanted us to go, he said. Me, little Morris and him.

He went to get our coats. I wrapped up Morris warmly. I lifted him up, up above my head. There he was, so beautiful, my own little baby boy. I lift him up and I say: Hello, Sammy.

A PORTRAIT

The security guard stood in room four of the main city gallery. He was looking intently at the portrait of the internationally acclaimed writer Frida Nowak. Frida Nowak, in the painting, was seated behind a table. She was in her early forties. She wore a grey buttonless cardigan, her brown hair tied back in a low bun.

What the gallery security guard saw was a woman leaning forward, an arm across an open book, a woman disquieted. Looking again, he ventured the thought that she was panicking.

*

'Hello, John,' Frida said.

He was her married part-time lover and literary agent. So much to take on.

She had looked up from her book. He was sober. Although it was difficult to be certain of this.

'I've stopped drinking,' he said.

This pronouncement alarmed her. When he was drunk, he was erratic. He would forget to turn up. On those occasions when he was sober, he was distant and looked unhealthy.

'I've started divorce proceedings,' he said.

'Oh,' she said.

She found it impossible to say more.

His wife, he had told her, was unscrupulous, as crazy as a fox. Don't believe a word she says, he'd said.

Soon after he left, John's wife, the actress Mariella Marfisi visited her. There was a knock on her door, and there she was, all in yellow, a capacious loose-fitting yellow summer dress and an extravagant wide-brimmed yellow hat.

'I hope you know what you're letting yourself in for,' Mariella said.

They had coffee together.

'It got too much for me,' she said. 'The drinking. And the other woman.'

'Other woman?'

'You, dear,' Mariella said.

'Oh. Oh, yes.'

'And the others.'

'The others?'

'The other women.'

'There were other women?'

'There still are, dear.'

'Other women?'

'Sheila. Have you met Sheila?'

'No.'

'Sheila works at the Institute of Contemporary Arts. All those excuses, those late nights at work. That was Sheila. It still is Sheila, why not? And Judith. You must know about Judith.'

'Judith?'

'God knows what John sees in her. She is huge, dear. The size of a baby elephant. Buttocks she can hardly get through a wide-open door. I've seen her. Not been introduced. But saw her with him going into a restaurant in Chiswick. Him and Judith. She wears this appalling perfume; you must have smelt it. It's on John's coat after he's been with her. Smells like burnt orange.'

'I – I thought that was yours.'

'Mine? God no. Mine? You must have thought me a dreadful old slag. Burnt orange, dear. Those perfumes he comes home with, apart from the booze, dear, the smell of those various women of his. Sweet horseradish – true – awful, quite, quite awful – the smell of sweet horseradish. And then there was you – there's you – I know when he's been with you. Well, what can one say, dear – lavender Eau de Cologne. I used to think, I wondered what you were like? Homely, one imagined. A quiet supper, the two of you, in front of the television. Well, I mustn't keep you, dear,' she said, and with that she rose. She had an appointment that afternoon with her solicitor.

'The divorce papers and all that,' she said as she left.

Frida's friend the gynaecologist Dr Anthony Lambert, viewing the portrait, said, 'Poor dear woman. A scholar, as we all know. An intellectual. But something missing, an inability to remain sane. Such a nice woman. Much loved by friends and the reading public. Wonderful writer. Modern. Incisive. Up there among the best. Not entirely accessible.'

At home, in the quiet of her bedroom, away from others, her mind turned cartwheels. Everybody making their demands, attempting to own her. Her doctor had said she must rest. Had prescribed antidepressants, this and that, none of which she cared to take, fearful they would undermine her imagination, her ambition. So they remained at the back of a drawer in her bedroom, hidden from John, who knew she had not been taking them but refrained from saying so. He did not like to interfere. He was hoping for another book from her. So was her publisher. A vulture sat upon her shoulder; the beak prepared to pluck out her brains.

'She had a miscarriage,' John told an old friend at his club. 'I said, come on, old girl, pull yourself together. Which wasn't very tactful, I suppose. What I meant was, as I said to her, we can have another go. Which afterwards I thought perhaps wasn't the best thing to say. It made her cry. She wasn't at her best when she cried. I know that sounds callous, but I've never really been any good with the pathetic. I don't know how to handle it. It makes me cross, irritated. I suppose a lot of men might feel the same. Anyway, I said I'm sorry, I am sorry. I said it several times. I am sorry, I said. Would you like a cup of tea? I said. It was the only thing that came to mind. She sat there at the table with a book. I don't know what it was she was reading. But she sat there, her mouth slightly open, wide eyed, tears welling up, her shoulders slumped. I went to the fridge, poured myself a beer. I had stopped drinking but the occasion called for a beer. Just one. Though later on I had another. I have to say I blame her. I'd made the effort, I'd stopped drinking and then she starts to cry, the tears in her eyes and that awful bloody look about her and I think just one, I must just have one, and once I'd had the one, I was back on the booze again. Christ. Then there was my wife. She'd been stirring it up, with her bitchy nonsense, making out that I had hundreds of women, loads of affairs. Some hope of that. So, there we are, Frida doesn't like me drunk, she doesn't like me sober, my wife turns her against me. And her publisher has been onto her night and day about her book.'

'How did you find her,' the police asked the cleaner.

'Asleep,' she said. 'There she was. I went into the bedroom. I'd called out, you see, but she didn't answer. I felt her wrist, but her heartbeat in her wrist wasn't there. So, I called the doctor. Sat by her side, by the side of the bed. And waited. I waited. I didn't know what to do. Then I phoned the police. Poor child. For that was what she was, so innocent, so sensitive. That's the trouble of course, sensitivity. Too much of it. Too fragile. God knows I never thought it'd come to this. But all those books, the reading, always reading, then the writing, always, always writing, up late at night working, reading, writing, overdoing it, that's my point. Not knowing when to give up, to take a break, as my husband would say. She was driven. Only, only the fact is, the poor woman hadn't the strength for it all, that's my belief. My husband said she was a bloody lunatic. No, she wasn't, I said. Don't you talk like that. She was different, that's all. Different from other people. She'd not got the strength. Too much bloody imagination for her own good, my husband said. Well, be that as it may, I said to him, she's given great pleasure to many people both in this Country and abroad, I said. Didn't do her much good though, did it, he snaps back. He's a builder.'

Two days before Frida Nowak took the overdose and killed herself her sister visited and brought along her child, a little girl, who, on her own, had opened the door and entered. Stood there watching, until Frida looked up and saw her.

'Come in,' she said to the child. 'No, you're not disturbing me. It's just a silly old book. Thomas Hardy. Actually it's rather good. I've read it already and I'm reading it again. So I know the story, well, the bones of it. There's so much more to Hardy than the first reading, I think. Anyway, enough of that, me prattling on. How nice to see you and who is that you've got? It's Teddy. Lovely Teddy. I don't think I had a teddy, but I had a monkey, a grey monkey which was nice. I liked monkey. I called him Monkey. Not very imaginative of me, was it? But that was who he was: Monkey. He was my best friend. Your Teddy is your friend. Monkey was mine. I told Monkey everything. Adults never seem to have the time to listen. I lost Monkey on the way. Oh, I don't know, I must have been about ten or eleven or something like that. I lost him. Goodness knows where he went. I suspect he went to a very good home. I lost him. And nothing was the same again. So, I began to write books and poems. When I write I am speaking to Monkey. That's how I write. It's Monkey and me. And it just comes out, dear. It comes out when I am speaking to him. And he says, good for you, keep going, love to hear some more, oh that's interesting, yes, I agree, and all that sort of thing. He's quite a bright monkey. But then, dear, he sometimes goes on holiday, sometimes for a long time, and then I miss him and can't write and things aren't the same, things go wrong. It's not a good time when he's away. And, and he's away more and more and for longer and longer these days, I'm afraid.'

She had been looking down at the table where she was sitting, and when she looked up again, the child had gone.

'This wonderful portrait of Frida Nowak,' the gallery director announced to the press and to the guests and gallery staff, 'has most kindly been donated to the gallery by the artist. It is a picture of a genius, a writer of immense talent, a woman who has contributed significantly to modern literature, indeed, to the culture of the nation. Her work will continue to be read for centuries; I might say for as long as there is civilization.'

The gallery security guard returned to the portrait.

'Looks to me,' he said to himself, 'the woman needed to get out in the fresh air. That's what she needed. All that reading and writing, it doesn't do no one any good. One can have too much of it. And that's a fact.'

'I don't think it looks much like her, to be honest,' Frida Nowak's cleaning woman said. 'They say her bloke, John, has gone back to his missus. These arty types, they're a rum lot, that's for sure.'

*

Four months after Frida Nowak's death, the portrait was stolen. News of its theft received prominent attention in the newspapers, on television and social media. There was speculation as to how the theft had been achieved and about the responsibility of the gallery's staff and management.

People from all over the country and from overseas gathered to look at the empty space where it had once hung, and which, for those viewing it, held a mystery and fascination of its own. There was a foreboding sense of loss, it was felt. An intimation of vacuity and exhaustion. Who was this woman? Why had she killed herself? They stood six-deep, looking intently and with wonder at the space where it used to be. Someone was heard to remark, 'Astonishing'

Underneath the space where the painting had hung, there was a bouquet of flowers along with a message which read 'Much missed'.

John and his wife Mariella visited the gallery to see what all the fuss was about.

'Give it time,' John said to her, 'someone will want to purchase it.'

'The painting?' Mariella said.

'The empty space,' John said.

'It's all rather sad,' they heard a woman near the front say.

'You can see where it used to be,' another woman said. 'The faintly dark lines round where the frame was.'

'What are we looking at,' a child asked.

'Where the portrait of Frida Nowak used to be, dear.'

'I can see it,' a woman standing nearby said.

'What?'

'The Frida Nowak. I can see it. Although it isn't there. It's left its imprint, its essence.'

'I can't see it,' the child said.

'How exasperating,' Mariella said. 'What are these people doing?'

'They're paying homage to Frida Nowak,' John said.

'They didn't know her. They don't know her like we did,' Mariella said.

'They think they do,' John said.

'No one really knew her,' Mariella said. 'Not even herself.'

'I could stand here all day,' a woman was heard to say.

'Nothing is lost,' a man at the back said.

*

After the portrait was found – it was discovered in a wheelie bin in East Wanstead – the gallery executive decided that, mindful of public interest, the empty space would remain and Frida Nowak's portrait would be displayed next to it.

'Well, she's certainly caused quite a story,' her cleaner said.

'There's not many who get the sort of attention she's getting now she's dead. All these people here queuing to see what isn't there. It's remarkable, that's what I say. Not that she'd have liked it at all. Not her. She wasn't one for this sort of thing, all this malarky. My husband Barry says as how they're taking the piss. The world's gone stark staring mad, he says. Lost touch with reality. That's the problem, he says, no one wants reality anymore. My husband's not one for the arts, not in the modern sense of the word.'

John, Mariella and Frida Nowak's sister decided Frida's funeral should be a private family affair. No fuss. No crowds.
'It would have been what she'd have wanted,' they agreed.

One morning, not long after the portrait and the empty space were first displayed, the gallery security guard found the dark smudged lines which contained the empty space were no longer visible. He looked, kept looking but, no, they'd gone. The thing what was there, he said, was missing.
'It's been stolen,' the management said.
People flocked to see where the empty space once had been.

ACROSS THE FIELDS

Looking across the countryside near Bougival, there is the tomato patch beneath the apple tree where a woman hangs out linen to air. There's the dog barking again. A bell ringing singularly at the old church. A light blue kindly sky.

Marie is meeting Tomas by the bridge on the other side of the village. The two of them are to be wed before the year is out. Marie's father sees no future in Tomas, the young man a clerk in the village post office. But love will prevail, that's what is said.

Anna is alone, when it comes to marriage. She has a club foot. She's a strong girl, can handle a horse, a straying cow as well as any man, apart from Pierre. Pierre is six feet six, built like an ox.

A slight breeze in the tops of the trees. These are ancient fields.

The woman hanging out the linen is a memory of Marguerite who died in childbirth five years ago, wife to Maurice Touler. After she died a space was created where now the woman can be seen hanging linen to air by the dead tree, by the wooden gate of the tomato patch that is beneath the apple tree, on whose branches the apples have begun to ripen.

THE SONG OF THE WIDOW, MRS WILLIAMS OF SOUTH ROAD, CROSBY

'Mrs Anwen Morris and her four children, such a pleasant respectable family. Caernarvon people. All in all, well-regarded members of the Welsh community and of Stanley Road Chapel,' Mrs Williams of South Road, Crosby, Liverpool, says to Gwenda, who is busily dusting Mrs Williams' front parlour.

'Captain Morris, Merchant Navy man, died at the end of last year, 1915, Gwenda. And they said it would all be over by Christmas, didn't they now? Him injured at sea. His ship torpedoed by one of them German U boats, off the Old Head of Kinsale. Died soon after coming home to Bootle. Now it's his wife Anwen Morris and their four children.'

'The eldest, Rhodri, sixteen years old, such a clever young man, quite outstanding, he is. Up there at the top of his class he was when he was at Bootle Grammar,' Mrs Williams is saying, she standing at the door of her front parlour, watching over Gwenda as she works.

'Of course,' she says, 'It's on him now to support his mother, support his brothers and his sister Megan. His mother arranged for him to attend an interview with the manager of the Midland Bank but he says the lad is too good for them, too good, Gwenda, can you believe? Wasted, the manager told his mother. He'd do better to apply for the Civil Service, take the exams. The boy has a future, he said. So now, I hear from his mother Mrs Morris, the young man is in the tax office in Liverpool. They say he can stay there, so he's near the family, take his exams, a great many exams by all accounts, then he'll have to transfer to Birmingham as they have more need of him there, in Birmingham, although, as I say, he can stay in Bootle, stay at home until the war is over and done with,' Mrs Williams says, says all in one breath – Gwenda dusting the bits and pieces on the mantelpiece.

'There's that Helen Tanner girl, Mrs Tanner's eldest, would like a slice of that young fellow, this according to his mother,' Mrs Williams says to Gwenda – Gwenda on her hands and knees cleaning the kitchen floor as she does every Tuesday afternoon. 'Helen Tanner working for the Liverpool branch of the Soldiers and Sailors Family Association. She's been turning up to tea at the Morris'. Turns up, invites herself in, partakes of the tea – the currant cake – slices so thin they are, you can read the Liverpool Echo through them. That's what Griffith, my husband's brother says, and it's no wonder, and no fault in that, times being as they are.'

'Mrs Morris' boy below Rhodri is on the violin. The youngest is on the piano, mad keen on the piano, his mother says. All day, whenever he can, fingers all over the piano keys. Sees himself a concert pianist, his mother tells me, my God. They're a musical family they are. Well, it's what you can expect being Welsh, music and the Welsh, it's in our blood, Gwenda,' Mrs Williams says. 'Not much peace and quiet in that household one can imagine, Gwenda. The violin and piano going hell for leather, all hours of the day. Mrs

Morris is made of strong material she is, has to be with those two boys and with their sister Megan who, Mrs Morris tells me, wants to be a teacher, like that Marjorie Evans girl at Clint Road Council School in Wavertree.'

'And there's Rhodri with his brains supporting the whole family, the lot of them, and thank God for him,' she says – Gwenda giving a final mopping over of the kitchen floor. 'Thank God someone's got brains, their father, Captain Morris, having passed away from this troubled life.'

'It only seems like it was yesterday,' she says – Gwenda giving a wipe of the kitchen surfaces, 'the boy Rhodri and his friend Thomas with their school caps on their heads, after school, after tea, out in the street playing football. Come seven o'clock, Thomas back inside to do his algebra, him struggling with the subject, and Rhodri out there on his own with the football, kicking it against the wall, backwards and forwards, till, come eight o'clock, he's back at home to his Mam. Home to Megan, to his brothers Evan and Morgan. Morgan, the youngest, is on the piano all hours of the day. He has a liking for a life in the theatre, his mother says.'

'Megan, she's a young woman now, turned fifteen she is; she's taller than their mother. I've seen her, her and Mrs Morris, only last week it was, outside Lewis' in Renshaw Street. There she is with her Welsh nose. There's no mistaking Megan, tall with that fine nose of hers. Evan's a good solid boy; stalwart his mother says of him. A good solid lad, not brilliant like Rhodri, but steady, thoughtful, 'middle-range' his teacher has said of him. And Rhodri now, him sixteen and close to seventeen. Too good he is, Mrs Morris, the manager at the Midland Bank says to the boy's mother. Too good for us. He's wasted. We're happy to have him here, make no mistake, Mrs Morris,' Mrs Williams again says to Gwenda, and it'll not be the last Gwenda will hear of it. 'But that lad, he's got what it takes for the Civil Service. The Civil Service exams, he'll have them under his belt with little trouble, that's my opinion. Have him put in for the Civil Service, for the Inland Revenue, him with his capacity for arithmetic, for mathematics in general, that's what the Midland bank manager said to Mrs Morris, Gwenda,' Mrs Williams says.

'Rhodri is quite the young man now he is, he's taken to smoking a pipe.' Mrs Williams tells Gwenda – Gwenda in the hallway, dusting the framed pictures of the late Mr Williams, pictured with the local cricket club team, then him, when he was just a young man, in the 98th Prince of Wales Regiment, looking all smart and proper along with the others in his army uniform, and there's the photo of him at The Cardiff and County Club Christmas Dinner 1902.

'Truth to tell,' Mrs Williams says, 'young Rhodri looks quite the man with the pipe stem between his teeth, the bowl nestled in the palm of his hand. And so it is, him in his utility dark grey suit, the tie, clean white shirt, polished black shoes as expected of him by his employers at the Liverpool Tax Office. Look at him, won't you, his Mam says to me when I see her and him outside Woolworth's in Church Street, quite the young fellow he is, quite the gentleman, and thank God for that. His father would be proud.'

'And there's Janice Jenkins, knock, knock on the front door,' Mr Williams says, transported, swept away, as she is, by her narrative. 'It's Janice Jenkins herself it is. There she is after school, after teaching all the day long. And is it Rhodri she wants to see now, is it? Is it Rhodri? It is, indeed it is, it's him and no other, Gwenda. Him and all his life before him. It's his life Janice Jenkins would be looking to, it would. It's his life and hers joined together in holy matrimony, she'll be hoping for, she'll be praying for, Gwenda. And here he is, it is him himself at the door. Janice Jenkins on the steps. The thin young man, you could play the harp on his rib cage, you could, him with no flesh on him. Him with his pipe in his hand. Is that you, Janice? he says. It's me, it is, Rhodri, she says. Is it a nice cup of tea you'd be wanting now? his mother says to Janice Jenkins. I'll not want to trouble you, Mrs Morris, she'll say, but in she'll go, she'll not say no to a cup of tea and a slice of Mrs Morris' currant cake, we can be sure of that, we can,' Mrs Williams says to Gwenda – Gwenda on her way up the stairs to do the bedrooms; Mrs Williams herself not able to follow after her, on account of her arthritic knees. All the way up there at night, and once down in the morning, is all she can manage now.

'Thank you, Gwenda, it all looks very nice, thank you. The money is on the hall side table. I'll be seeing you next Tuesday then, shall I?' Mrs Williams says to Gwenda who is back downstairs again, has on her coat and is all ready to leave.

'The new couple who've moved into Hyde Road, the husband, Major Corstair-Berton has been discharged from the army, so Mrs Carter, who lives next door to them, was telling me, Gwenda. He's been up to no good, by all accounts,'

But Gwenda is down the path, off to her home in Linton Street, there to get the tea on the table for her husband Robert and their two boys.

Old Mrs Williams closes her front door; her narrative regarding the misconduct of Major Corstair-Berton of Hyde Road to be deferred until the following Tuesday afternoon.

In her hallway she runs a finger, finding dust, along the top of the framed pictures of her late husband at The Cardiff and County Club Christmas Dinner 1902, and of him with the 98th Prince of Wales Regiment.

*

'Look at him now, won't you?' Mrs Williams cries out to Gwenda at the photo of young Rhodri in his Civil Service suit and tie, his white shirt, laundered and pressed no doubt at the Dry Cleaners local to where he now lived in Small Heath, Birmingham.

For he was not now living at home with his Mam and brothers and sister in Gonville Road, Bootle, although one could be sure he sent money home to keep them to the standard of living they'd come to expect.

'Mrs Morris tells me Rhodri is in lodgings now,' Mrs Williams says to Gwenda. 'Nice bedroom, small parlour, bathroom shared with one other. Breakfast at seven thirty and tea at six in the dining room downstairs served by the landlady's daughter, by the name of Veronica. She'd best watch herself, that Veronica, best put behind her all thoughts of looking to a future with that young man in his suit, his boots polished. I'd tell her, I would, he's not for you, lass. Our Rhodri is set for higher things, him with his brains, his courteous demeanour, his careful ways. No one can dispute it.'

'If ever there was a young man to be relied upon, to meet all necessary qualifications it is Mrs Morris' Rhodri, him all of twenty-nine years now,' Mrs Williams says to Gwenda who is polishing the kitchen floor before going on to dust-and-do for Mrs Carter in Mount Street.

'It seems only the other day that young man Rhodri Morris was in his short pants playing football against the wall along with his boyhood friend Thomas who I hear has taken a position with Littlewoods,' she says to Gwenda on her knees over by the cooker that Mrs Williams bought only last November from Blacklers on the corner of Elliot Street. 'Such a nice lad, that Thomas,' she says.

'Always so willing, so good natured, but not academic in any sort of way, so his Mam tells me. He knew how to kick a football with young Rhodri, young boys as they were, and into the evening as the light began to fail, but, sure as sure, he hasn't had the brains as has Rhodri. It takes all sorts,' Mrs Williams says to Gwenda now wiping the kitchen surfaces.

As proudly recounted to Mrs Williams by the young man's mother, there was Rhodri of an evening in his lodgings with his favourite book, a Dorothy Sayers, a Ronald Knox detective novel or an Anthony Trollope. Friday nights he'd go to the pub for a half, hurry over to the tennis and social club, meet up there for a game and a pint. Young Mr Morris was doing well, they said at the Birmingham Branch. Solid, reliable, conscientious. Word had it, in time, he could be transferred to Bury as Assistant Manager. They'd be sorry to lose him, Mrs Morris had said.

His brother Morgan, the youngest boy, was in the theatre, Mrs Morris told Mrs Williams in Owen Owens in Clayton Square. My God, that was no surprise, although the whole family had been against it, theatre life being an uncertain occupation, the cost of living being what it was, and businesses all over closing their doors, people struggling to keep up, not knowing where the next penny was to be coming from.

'It's a terrible time for so many of us,' Mrs Williams had said to Gwenda who had lost her employment with Mrs Carter in Mount Street, Mrs Carter herself saying she was having to economise like most of them round those parts.

Mrs Williams would herself be keeping Gwenda on, she had said to her, although there had been plenty of women and girls out there who had been desperate for employment. And hadn't Mrs Williams herself, she said, not had one or two of them knocking on her door, offering to do the work at half what they'd get in better days. But Gwenda was in need of the work, with her husband Robert crippled with his back as he had been, having to lay out on his bed for more time during the blessed day than otherwise would have been considered normal. Gwenda knew the job, knew what was what, and Mrs Williams had got used to her, she coming Tuesdays, week in, week out all those years. So, she could stay on, she had said to Gwenda, her sweeping out the hallway beneath the framed photographs of the late Mr Williams pictured, as Mrs Williams had so informed Gwenda on more occasions than Gwenda could have recalled, with the local cricket club team, and then him, a young man in the 98th Prince of Wales Regiment. And there was the picture of the late Mr Williams looking all smart and proper in his army uniform, and there he was again at The Cardiff and County Club Christmas Dinner 1902, at the end of which year, Christmas 1902, he passed away, his heart giving up and him being just fifty-three years old. Very sudden on the kitchen floor, it had been, she told Gwenda. It had been on the very same kitchen floor, she said, which Gwenda had been cleaning Tuesday afternoons since she started working for her all those years ago.

She and her husband, Mrs Williams told Gwenda, had left Caernarvon in her young thirties in 1889, had come to live in Crosby to be close to his mother, his father being on the ships like Mrs Morris' husband Captain Morris. When they were in Caernarvon, she and her husband had a house not far from Morfa Common Park, and she had heard Lloyd George speak, a great orator he was, 'a man of the people'. A year after they came to Crosby their son David, nine years old he had been, passed away, quite sudden from pneumonia. It had been a terrible thing. It broke her husband's heart, she said. He'd not hear the boy's name but the tears would come into his eyes. He was a fine lad. Fair hair, like his Da. Very promising, thought of highly, the school remarking, as they had, on his academic progress, and he had such a smile, he had, such a way, such a liveliness. She didn't much speak of him and his passing, she had tucked it away. It'd been the way she managed, she said, and she'd not spoke of him to anyone not in recent times, only to Gwenda on that one occasion, her being part of the family, so to speak, as she had told Mrs Morris in the bakery at the Lyons State Café.

'Mrs Morris' youngest Morgan is at the Playhouse,' Mrs Williams says to Gwenda.

He was helping out, working at the backstage business, his Mam had said to Mrs Williams at Lewis'. 'They tell him he'll have his chance at the acting as such, small parts at first, during the forthcoming season of plays. They'll be doing Shakespeare's Macbeth,' Mrs Morris had said.

She had heard a London actor had been engaged for the title role, she'd not ever seen him herself but he was held up highly throughout the Country and America too she'd read in The Echo with a picture of him as King Lear and another one of him as Othello and they said in life he was not a tall man at all, quite the opposite, on the short side like Mr Tanner the butcher back of Merton Street, but then he'd stand up there on the stage, not Mr Tanner, the actor playing Othello, and one would think he was six feet tall, even taller, a powerful figure of a man who, by all accounts, one couldn't keep one's eyes off.

Mrs Morris' young Morgan would have a long way to go before

he could show himself the like. One could only hope, his Mam had said, he would manage to make a living from it at all, have enough behind him, him with wife and family whenever he might or not get round to having a wife and family, although he'd not be considered much of a catch, not if he didn't rise in the ranks or take up some other more secure employment and there was his Uncle Berwyn willing to take him on at his hardware in Hawthorne Road.

'Each to his own,' Mrs Morris had said to Mrs Williams.

*

'Rhodri hasn't heard when he's to be transferred to the tax offices in Bury St Edmunds as yet,' Mrs Williams says to Gwenda. 'I met Mrs Morris outside Lewis' in Ranelagh Street. She said Rhodri probably wouldn't know till later in the year.'

According to Mrs Morris, Rhodri was settling down well there in Birmingham, she says to Gwenda. He attended the summer festival in Cannon Hill Park in Edgbaston on Saturday. Everyone was there apparently – employees from Rhodri's tax office building and local companies, the Birds Custard factory, BSS over at Small Heath, the Rover Plant in Longbridge, Typhoo Tea, goodness knows, the whole world, such an occasion it had been, a yearly event. All sorts of activities and competitions, Mrs Morris had told her. Rhodri and a colleague from the Tax office went in for the sack race, she said, and they very nearly won, only they were pipped at the post by two young ladies who worked in administration at the HP Sauce factory in Aston, and later on that evening Rhodri and his colleague accompanied the two young ladies to the social club. Quite the high-life by the sounds of it, Mrs Morris had said to her.

'Proud as punch she was,' Mrs Williams said to Gwenda.

'I hear from Mrs Morris Rhodri is walking out with the young lady he had met at Edgebaston summer Festival. Her name is Julia. Julia Walker,' Mrs Williams says to Gwenda, her turning up as ever on time Tuesday afternoon. 'He's brought her home to Bootle and Mrs Morris says she's very nice, very presentable. It seems Rhodri is much taken with her, he is. Quite the attentive suitor. She's the young lady he met at the Edgbaston summer festival and who is with the HP Sauce factory in Aston, Mrs Morris tells me. By all accounts, she's secretary to one of the company's executives. HP Sauce itself, Mrs Morris said, is of course very well established. Known throughout the Nation and beyond. She tells me she'd not previously bought HP Sauce herself, has never tasted it, but, Julia being with HP Sauce and secretary to one of the top executives, she tells me she has now bought a bottle from Church Street and added a little to the side of her and her boys' plates of lamb stew and, she said, it is very nice, a nice good bodied sauce, it is, and one to be proud of. Although her daughter Megan hadn't quite taken to it, not as yet, but Mrs Morris was sure in time she'd acquire the taste. HP Sauce, she said, was a sauce one 'got to know', so to speak, she said.'

'Rhodri's Julia will do well by him,' Mrs Williams says to Gwenda. 'Rhodri's Julia is the lucky one, she is, although Mrs Morris says there's not been talk as such of a wedding at this present time. Mrs Morris is not one to push her hopes for them further than she considers appropriate. They must be the ones to decide. Although Mrs Morris herself,' Mrs Williams says, 'is full to the top of her head of expectation with regard to the matter.'

*

It was a splendid occasion, the wedding of Rhodri and Julia at St

Bartholomew's, Edgbaston, Mrs Williams reports to Gwenda, as had been the reception at the Social and Tennis Club. She didn't attend herself, Mrs Williams says, the arthritis having taken a turn for the worst, the pain down the right leg and in both her knees having a field-day, she could hardly put one foot after the other, so she hadn't gone but had heard all about it from Mrs Morris herself, who looked the picture of happiness, and so she ought, Rhodri happily married and the two of them, he and Julia, Mr and Mrs Morris now, residing in a well-appointed first floor flat in Edgbaston. Spacious it is, Mrs Morris had said. Large 'lounge' in the front, a quiet road too, bedroom, separate kitchen, bathroom of their own, plentiful cupboard space, she had said. His wife, Julia, was continuing at HP Sauce for the present, while they settled, to help things out, the cost of living being what it was, and the rent a significant expense, but that was to be expected in Edgbaston and it was Edgbaston where one would expect Rhodri and Julia to live, at least for the time being, until they purchased their own property, which, given Rhodri's position and qualifications, his courteous manner and commitment to the task in hand, one could expect them to do before so very long,' Mrs Williams says.

She understood from Mrs Morris that Rhodri's Julia had told her that Rhodri had proposed to Julia at the 1st Test Match, England versus Australia at Trent Bridge after, Mrs Williams seemed to remember Mrs Morris saying, Jack Hobbs had been caught and bowled out for 78.

*

'One would have thought the war, 1914-1918, was supposed to be the war to end all wars. That's what people said, in the papers and all over,' Mrs Williams says to Gwenda. 'And here we are at war again with Germany, our lads there in France and everywhere. Liverpool, all about the docks bombed, devastated, it's here in the Echo.'

Gwenda places Mrs Williams' tea on her bedside table.

Mrs Williams is in her eighties, plagued with arthritis, her legs almost good for nothing, age having got her by the neck as she has said of it, said of it on a regular basis, and her with a troublesome heart, her breathing all over the place. So it is that she stays the mornings in bed until Gwenda comes soon after twelve, to wash her down where it matters, help her dress, goes with her carefully step by step to the downstairs 'lounge', there Mrs Williams calling out to her from time to time, commenting on the news in the Liverpool Echo, on the neighbours, on Mrs Morris and her family, while Gwenda is about the cleaning of the kitchen and the vacuuming of the carpets in the front hallway with Mrs Williams' brand new Hoover Upright Vacuum Cleaner.

Gwenda goes back home in Linton Street to get the tea. Then returns seven o'clock to get Mrs Williams, 'the Duchess' as Gwenda has come to speak of her, and not without affection, back upstairs to her bed again. That's how it has become.

'Mrs Morris dropped round this morning,' Mrs Williams calls from the 'lounge'. 'She'd heard at chapel about my legs and my heart and that. Very good of her. Quite unexpected it was. She tells me that Rhodri and his wife and their two boys are in London now. Rhodri working in London, excused from army service, him having important work in the civil service. Nice house they've got, she said. Though the doodlebugs are flying there overhead and one never knows when they're coming down on one. Rhodri's wife

Julia, Mrs Rhodri Morris, evacuated with the boys to Merioneth, stayed near elderly relatives it seems. Only she couldn't stand it, she said, missed her husband, felt out of it, stayed in Merioneth just five days it was, then back to London she went. Her Rhodri at work in the city all day and fire-fighting at night, the poor man must be exhausted, well, everyone is, with the bombs and the shortages. And Julia sneaks down to the market, somewhere she knows, brings back cherries for the boys waiting for her in the bomb shelter in the back garden as they have there, the cherries a proper treat, so Mrs Morris tells me. Mrs Morris herself is not a well woman, and her not yet seventy, Gwenda. Age is a terrible thing, it is, that's for sure. It gets you by the scuff of the neck it does, it's got Mrs Morris, Rhodri's mam, in her back, got it in her joints, her bones. She'd been to stay a few days with them, Easter time, very nice she said. Nice little garden, on a slope, a few vegetables, cabbages and that down at the back, and the boys are very pleasant, proper little gentlemen she said, and the younger one, the fair-haired lad, top of his class at school like our David, asking questions what it was they were saying, Rhodri and his mam talking Welsh in the back garden with the daffodils all out, the bluebells on their way. And the front wall taken away for the metal. All along the road. They've got a car too, a Wolseley, green it is, although there's no petrol, not when you want it, the same as everywhere.'

THE ACCIDENT

She is well out of it now. It all happened over twenty years ago. The accident; the death as she sometimes thinks of it when she gets low. The boy at the side of the road. His body.

She was on the phone to Mathew but he didn't answer. She tried twice, three times. She texted. She phoned the police. She waited by his side. He was twelve, maybe thirteen. She found him, she said. She said she was driving along; she saw him lying there. She thought, she prayed he might be alive. The ambulance took him to the hospital. Should she go with him? No, they said. They'd got her address and phone number. Mathew phoned. She told him she found the boy. He had taken a cab, and drove her home. Her body was shaking. It was the shock, he said. He handed her a large brandy which she picked up in the bathroom. She took a pill. He tucked her up and she fell asleep.

The police call round the next day. She tells them the same story. They send someone round to have a look at the car. Mathew says they do that with all the cars known to have travelled that road at about that time of night. The cameras record them.

What's the damage on the off-side front panel? they ask. She hit a tree. She saw the body and swerved, lost control and hit a tree, she tells them.

They arrest three kids. Two black, one white. There was dope in the car. They hadn't a driving licence. There was damage to its off-side front wing.

Mathew says let's get out of here. Let's take off. He can work from wherever, he says. Thank God for the internet, he says. He's on his guard. His jaw is set. I think we ought to stay, she says, at least until everything is sorted. No, he shouts. He shouts. He knows. She's sure he knows. They have a house in Ireland outside Glenmore in County Kilkenny.

She didn't see him. She tells him. She has to tell him. They're leaving, going to Glenmore and she has to tell him somehow. He stands there. They're in the living room. She wishes he'd sit down. She has said 'sit down'. But he doesn't; he remains standing by the window. She's in the armchair by the stereo.

She takes a breath. She tells him. It was dark. It could have happened to anyone. It was the corner, the bend in the road. She didn't think she was speeding. It all happened so quickly, all in a moment. She didn't know she'd hit him, she says.

She had been on her way home from Anthea and Tom's leaving party in Sudbury Hill. Anthea and Tom were going back to Melbourne, Australia. Mathew wasn't there. He had to wait for a call from his office in Canary Wharf. He'd sent his love to the hosts. She'd taken a leaving present, a picture by Silvia Paul, an oil painting. She had been anxious in case she had chosen the wrong parting gift. But Anthea and Tom were delighted. Loved it. Thank you so, so much, Olivia, they said again and again. Everyone was there, apart from Mathew. They had been very sorry he hadn't been able to come, they said and said again and again. Everyone there, Tilly Maynard, the Garsons, Gerry and Tina, all of them said they'd all miss dear Anthea and Tom when they went back to Melbourne.

Don't drink too much, Mathew had said to her before she'd left for the party. And she hadn't. Just two Campari's and soda. And a lot of ice, she had said when she had got back to the house. She could have phoned for a cab, he said, which made her angry. It had been such a stupid inconsiderate thing to say. She had two Camparis, she had shouted. The bloody man. She was tired, that's all, she had said. She'd shouted because she had been tired and it'd been the shock.

Mathew is standing by the window. He hasn't said a word. She could do with a word or two, just something, him there, like he thinks he's the Rock of Gibraltar. What was the boy doing out there at that time of night? she says to him. And what, for God's sake, were his parents thinking? They've got something to answer for. Letting him out and on his own like that. It was crazy. They had some responsibility in this. It ought to be straightforward, she says. The boy in the dark. The bend in the road. It was an accident. Of course, it was, darling, he says. He's spoken at last. What else could he say.

We're leaving, Mathew says. He stands with his back to her now, looking out of the bay windows at the garden although it's dark out there. He can't see anything. He stands there, the man she's been married to for seven years, and look at him, he needs to smarten himself up, she says to herself.

She can't sleep at night. She can't eat. She drinks too much.

I'm not leaving, she says, says it in a voice louder than she intends.

She is leaving. Going to stay in their house in Glenmore. But she isn't going before she says she isn't. That's something she owes herself. She isn't going to be pushed around. She has to stand her ground. She has to hold onto herself.

She is taking with her the Sherree Valentine Daines' painting of the girls dancing. It makes no difference whether she ought to and, according to Mathew, she oughtn't. There's no room in the car, he says. She changes her mind about the girls dancing. It's her prerogative. She wraps the figurine the Lladro Angel in newspaper and tucks it between her underwear. She is taking the figurine. She'll not tell Mathew. As far as the figurine and she are concerned, Mathew is persona non grata. What about the cleaner? she says. They have to pay the cleaner. It's all been seen to, Mathew says.

She's being taken care of. She's being protected. She's to stay in the house near Glenmore, he says, with friends nearby, not so far away, Sheila and Gary Comber. She doesn't like Sheila and Gary Comber, she never has, but she doesn't say.

He drives the two hundred and forty-three miles to Pembroke Dock, then the four hours on the ferry to Rosslare, and from Rosslare he drives the thirty-five miles on the N25 to Glenmore. She doesn't drive. She could drive. But, he says, for the time being, he'll do the driving. She knows what he's implying. But she doesn't say. They drive in silence, because he doesn't speak. It's his habit not to speak when driving, he's a 'one thing at a time' man, the man she married seven years ago after they met at the Hurlingham Club and had been going steady for six months. He isn't the man to rush things, he's a man, she soon discovered, who prefers to deliberate, and once he has come to a decision, he moves on it unwaveringly.

She had always been a lively girl. A bright child. She had married well, they said, as they expected she would. They had tried for a child. She liked that, the idea of a child of their own, and

Mathew seemed to expect that in due course, as a matter of fact, a child would have been born to them. She had a miscarriage. Then nothing. And nothing.

The house outside Glenmore looks different. Even though she and Mathew visit at least once a year during the months of August, it isn't any longer recognizable as her own. Not entirely. There's the furniture, the paintings, the Barclay Butera Interiors Grey Colony sofas, Madison Park armchairs, the walnut tray tables, the antique beige faux silk taffeta curtains at the French windows. There's the garden beyond the French windows, the rhododendrons, the magnolia, the cherry blossom tree which has always been her favourite, the fuchsias, geraniums, white jasmine, honeysuckle, viburnum, the climbing roses. As a whole, though, the house and garden doesn't seem to her to be the same as it has been.

The morning after they arrive Sheila and Gary Comber call over and at once it becomes clear to her that she really likes them. It's like the old days. But better. She is no longer irritated by them, by their being too cheerful, as if they're making an effort to be so, to appear jolly and all very friendly. She must re-join the Waterford Golf Club, Sheila says. Of course, she had quite forgotten. The Waterford, Mathew. She was going to re-join, she says, as if, it seems to her, asking his permission.

It takes time, Mathew says to her before he goes back to London. He says he was hoping he could work a few days a week from Glenmore, but head office has informed him he needs to come in, there being reorganization and that sort of thing to attend to.

His departure leaves her feeling relieved, a burden has been lifted. She telephones the Waterford. It's so easy. She telephones Betty Langridge whose husband Jackson died from bowel cancer eighteen months ago. She arranges for Betty to pick her up, and drive them to the Butler Gallery in the historic Evans' Home in Kilkenny to see the O'Malley Collection and to view the exhibition of paintings by Daisy Smith and have a light lunch in the café. Betty is sweet and full of life and the exhibition is lovely. Absolutely fascinating. It would have been nice if Mathew could have been there with her and Betty, she says when later she phones him at work. Although, on reflection, she becomes aware that it was better without him.

She and Betty, Sheila and Gary Comber and a friend of theirs called Nadia visit the Woodstock Gardens outside Inistioge. Mathew has come over for a few days so he is able to join them. Wonderful walks, Betty says. The beautiful rose garden, Sheila says. She loves the arboretum, the trees from all over Asia and everywhere. Everyone agrees, it's a lovely day.

During his stay Mathew is preoccupied. She can tell. She knows him. He is 'absent', 'elsewhere'. And she can't wait for him to leave. On his last day, he says he's to be transferred to Berlin for a few weeks, maybe longer. 'Orders from above' is what he says. Of course, he'd love for her to accompany him – 'accompany', she notes the words 'accompany' – but it's best she remains in Ireland. 'Remains' – so formal. She doesn't ask him why she shouldn't 'accompany' him, why she should 'remain'. She knows the reason why. She's pretty certain she knows. He's with another woman.

She telephones Betty, telephones Sheila and Gary, telephones Carol she met at the Golf Club. She goes with them to the Castle Howell, and then to Nore Valley, has lunch at The Fig Tree. On another day they go to Wexford, and then to the Lady's Island Lake and the seaside at Rosslare.

That Autumn the house in the UK is sold.

That was over twenty years ago. The kids in the car were discharged. She and Mathew have been divorced and he has married again. Her friends say she leads such a busy life. She has such energy. They don't know, they say, where she gets it from.

She gets a letter from England with the single word 'Justice' on it. And she gets two silent phone calls. She phones Mathew in Paris where he is now living, and he says she ought to have it checked out.

The cherry blossom is in full bloom.

She doesn't venture into the garden after nightfall.

PIG'S KNUCKLE, NEW YORK

OK, we're sitting here. And she's not talking to me. We're in Joey's. Up at the counter. Pig's Knuckle, Veal Cutlets, Boiled Beef. Right now, she's drinking coffee. I've got tuna sandwich and coffee. She's wearing that brown felt hat with the bow at the front. Why she wears that, I don't know. It doesn't suit her. She's blonde, she'd do better in a light straw affair, something uplifting. The brown job looks shabby, makes her look downbeat. Her name is Sheila. She works at Cooney's bookstore, at the back, on the accountings. I wander in there, I say, Hi, Sheila, lunch? She shrugs, pulls on her coat, it's blue. It's cold out, got to tuck yourself up good and proper, I say. I don't need to say, she's pulling the coat on, she's been outside, for God's sake, that's what she's saying in the way she's pulling on that blue coat.

The man sitting on the other side of her in Joey's is Sidney Tapter who did seven years inside for the job at Sumpsters Jewellers in Sefty Street. Sidney is a regular. He sits at the same place, his place at the counter between 12 and 2 every day, bar Sunday. Sunday he's laying flowers at his mother's grave. He's a good boy. In his mother's eyes he did no harm, did nothing wrong to no one. Quote, unquote. Sheila in her brown felt hat knows Sidney in passing, so to speak. He comes in the bookshop to read the papers. No one ever suggests he buy any of the books. It's Sidney, did seven years for the jeweller's job. Every man and woman have their bad luck stories. Not everyone can be Al Capone, someone said to Sidney. That about summed it up. Sheila reckons lunch at Joey's is Sidney's one and only meal of the day. So, when he's in the bookshop, let him read the papers.

The fella back of us, by the side of the tea urns, the cups and so on is Chaffy MacGuire, detective inspector. He's waiting nicely for Sidney to finish up his spaghetti and meat balls. He's waiting, in no hurry, not Chaffy. Then when the clock strikes two and Sidney starts to shift himself on his stool, over he comes. Sidney, he says, we'd like a word with you. OK. And that's how it goes. We're in Joey's, Sheila in her brown felt hat with the brown bow, on her second coffee and the glass of water, and I'm waiting for her to buck up, come out of the doldrums, girl. And there's Sidney off with Chaffy on account of the Dandy Street robbery last night, not that Sidney had anything to do with it, but Sidney was seven years inside for the Sumpsters job, so Sidney has to face the questioning, provide an alibi if he can find one. And there's nothing one can do, not me, not Sheila, not Joey himself. That's how it goes. You do time, you get pulled in. Your life's not your own no more.

FABRICS

Women leaning forward over fabrics, plain and flowered, greens and blacks, all afternoon till early evening when it was: 'That's it, ladies,' from Valerie the proprietor. Daisy, the youngest, only seventeen, her fingers aching, is first on her feet. Then Marjorie who is forty-five going on fifty. She has a husband to go to, a man who likes his dinner promptly at eight. Cecilia the French woman, who has been with Valerie for these fifteen years, has a cat with similar expectations regarding punctuality. If asked did they enjoy their work, they would have replied, should they have replied, that this was the place with which they identified. They came to this place, they cut and sewed fabrics under Valerie's watchful eye from eight-thirty till six, a long day, but one in which they were secured from the uncertainties and violence out beyond the walls of the room in which they worked.

LOOKING FOR JOAN

David Partiker arrived at Claudia Richardson's house in South Kensington. He was wearing his late wife's green puffer coat over her dark turtleneck jumper, a leopard-print blue cotton scarf and straight blue jeans.

As he entered Claudia's spacious living room, he was handed a red rose.

'Please do keep it safely with you for the duration of the meeting, Mr Partiker,' Claudia Richardson said.

Apart from himself and Claudia, there were six women and two men of the ages between forty-five and seventy.

No comment was made regarding his female attire.

During the preceding week, David had telephoned Claudia Richardson. He had told her he had been reading his late wife Joan's diary, and had discovered that at one time she had attended one or two of Claudia's 'Raising of World Consciousness' Group meetings.

He said he missed her greatly, and would very much like to attend a meeting should that be considered appropriate.

Claudia, recalling Joan, said she was sorry to hear of her passing, and that David would be most welcome to come along to the meeting to be held on the following Tuesday evening.

'Allow me to introduce you to Arnold Bilkin,' Claudia said to David of a tall thin man in his sixties.

She introduced him to Bret Dantine, an American, who, Claudia announced, 'has most kindly agreed to give us a talk after tea and biscuits.'

David sat himself on a large sofa next to a woman who, he observed, was wearing a black and white polka-dot dress which, he decided, had seen better days. Her name, she told him, was Beryl Jackson.

'We're all very concerned this evening with the whale,' she informed him ominously. 'The whale in the Hudson River. You must surely have heard about it. You may remember some years ago a whale, poor thing, got stuck in the Hudson River; caused quite a furore. Well, it's happened again. Not the same whale. One hopes not. A different one in all probability. But no less tragic. It seems that there have been quite a number of whales that have been stranded recently.'

'You know the Hudson River in the U.S of A?' asked an emaciated woman in the armchair next to the sofa where David was seated.

'I'm Lalla Dickon,' she said. 'What has happened is quite dreadful. Heartrending.'

'We are going to pray for it,' Claudia Richardson announced.

'Such a terrible thing to happen to the poor creature,' a full-figured woman in a capacious green shirt and cardigan said.

'It's frightening,' declared another. 'It's a tragedy.'

'Is the creature male or female?' the tall thin Arnold Bilkin enquired.

'No one, as far as we know, has been in a position to ascertain, Arnold,' Claudia said.

Claudia was waving her red rose.

'Ladies and gentlemen, shall we begin? As you know,' she said, 'we have a visit this evening by David Partiker. His dear wife, Joan, some of you may remember, joined us for a short while a few years ago. Joan passed away last year, and I know all of us offer our sincere condolences to David. We shall start, as we always do, with the circulation of the candle and our own personal dedications, shall we?'

A small lit candle was handed from one member of the group to another, who, as each in turn momentarily held it before them, dedicated the evening to that which was uppermost in their minds. Most of the dedications were to the whale in the Hudson, although the woman in the armchair next to where David was sitting said that, if no one objected and didn't think she was being greedy, she would like to dedicate the evening to 'World Peace and the whale'. The American guest of honour Bret Dantine, who was to give the talk, dedicated the evening to 'The Moment', which prompted a general murmur of appreciation and eager anticipation.

David was uncertain as to what or to whom he should make his dedication. When it came to his turn, he held the candle for longer than he feared was acceptable, and, in a rush, unable to order his thoughts, muttered: 'The whale, I suppose.'

'Good for you,' someone called.

'I shall now read from the list of Absent Friends,' Claudia announced. 'The list, David, is made up of those of our members who, for one reason or another, have been prevented from attending, and of others known to us who deserve our thoughts and prayers.'

The list was long and, it seemed to David, took an interminable length of time to complete.

Of the names read out, there were a number which were met with comments from members, such as 'Oh, I thought he'd long been dead'. And 'Oh dear, the poor woman'. Others were 'Goodness me, is he still with Muriel?', 'Those two are not what they would like people to believe them to be' and 'He once sold me a very nice eighteenth-century corner table.'

After the woman wearing the black and white polka-dot dress and whose name was Beryl Jackson had remarked of one of the named couples 'I pity their poor children', David became aware that the tall thin man by the name of Arnold Bilkin was winking at him.

'It is customary now for us to close our eyes and observe a few minutes of silence, David. This to be followed by a little prayer,' Claudia said.

'Oh, good,' David heard himself say.

David, together with the others, shut his eyes and waited for the ordained period of silence to end. After several minutes, it had failed to do so. Uncertain as to whether or not it was still in progress, he opened his eyes, and discovered Arnold Bilkin was again winking at him.

Thankfully, when in public, David had found that there had been markedly little reaction of an unpleasant nature with regard to him wearing Joan's clothes. One afternoon, while walking in the park, a small boy had approached him and asked if he was a man or woman. I'm a man, he had told the boy. These are my wife's clothes. She died a year ago, and sometimes I find it nice, well, reassuring, if you get my meaning, to wear her clothes. The boy hadn't seemed in any way troubled by that. His parents had beckoned to him, had leant down and spoken to the boy. They had looked over at David, and then had moved on.

Not wishing to acknowledge Arnold Bilkin's persistent winking, David closed his eyes. As he did so, he heard Claudia Richardson leading the prayers, in which she asked the Good Lord to have mercy on their poor souls, and to save the whale, which she explained to the Almighty was stranded in The Hudson River, and which most recently had been sighted swimming south of the Verrazano Bridge, which, she reminded Him, connects the boroughs of Brooklyn and Staten Island, and which is approximately two miles from the Statue of Liberty. Having furnished the Good Lord with detailed instructions as to the estimated location of the whale, Claudia announced, 'And now, we'll have tea and biscuits. After which, Bret Dantine shall deliver his Talk.'

Her announcement gave rise to heartfelt applause, both for the tea and biscuits and for Bret Dantine's anticipated contribution to the proceedings.

Tea and biscuits served and completed, Bret Dantine, remaining in the corner of the living room where he had sat throughout the evening, began speaking in a quiet, unwavering monotone of the power of The Moment, encouraging the group to focus their attention on that moment in which each of them even as he spoke was engaged. To aid them in this exercise, he suggested each mark with a pen or a biro a small cross on the fold of muscle between the thumb and forefinger, and, having done so, to focus their attention exclusively upon it. This instruction gave rise in the group to much fussing and small stifled yelps of panic as members put down their cups and saucers and sought to find their biros or borrow from one another.

'And as you concentrate on the cross between your thumb and forefinger,' Bret droned, 'you are finding that nothing else other than the cross is of importance to you and you are allowing the cross to lead you into your Centre where lies the Spiritual Knowledge which you are seeking. And now all doubt and confusion are falling away as one experiences Stillness, Oneness, Peace and Calm. And so it is, that one is now feeling calmer and calmer and calmer.'

It was at this early stage in Bret Dantine's talk that, lulled by Bret Dantine's colourless and unvarying delivery and overwarm in his late wife Joan's turtleneck jumper, David drifted off to sleep. He awoke to hear Claudia conveying her heartfelt thanks to Bret.

'That was so interesting,' Beryl Jackson said.

'I quite lost myself in it,' someone exclaimed.

'You see,' Claudia said to David, 'spiritual journeys are not always tempestuous and fraught with struggle and uncertainty. That is why I asked Bret here again tonight.'

David thought he had never felt so tired in all his life.

The South Kensington 'Raising of World Consciousness' Group meeting over, everyone was preparing to take their leave, when the woman in the grey top and slacks returned from the upstairs toilet.

'My friend has just phoned,' she announced. 'The whale in the Hudson River is dead.'

All present felt the whale's fate as if it was their own.

David observed that the heavily bosomed woman in the capacious green shirt and cardigan looked suicidal.

The goodbyes were muted.

'Don't forget to eat your roses,' Claudia reminded everyone. 'They're made of rice paper,' she said to David.

'Eat it, eat it, David,' someone said.

'Peppermint flavour,' David announced.

'We always eat the roses,' Claudia assured him.

'Your wife only came the once,' Claudia said to David as he stood in the hallway ready to leave. 'To be frank, we didn't feel we were able to aid her in finding what it was she might have been looking for. She laughed rather a lot.'

'Thank you so much for coming,' she called to everyone as they left the house.

As he walked to South Kensington Tube Station, he was joined by Beryl Jackson.

'I'm so sorry to hear about your wife,' she said. Then added: 'I do like your blue leopard-print scarf.'

They walked on a little further.

'It's very sad about the whale, isn't it?' she said. 'Mind you,' she confided, 'some of us on the committee knew the poor creature had been dead since this morning. But we decided not to say. We had already notified everyone that the whale in the Hudson would be the focal point of today's meeting. And we felt that to have told them in advance that the poor creature was already dead would have had a most detrimental effect upon the meeting. Once an agenda has been decided, Claudia and I think it's best not to change it in any significant way. I'm sure you agree.'

At the Underground station entrance she said, 'How did you like Arnold Bilkin? He lost his mother last year. It's hit him badly, I'm afraid. You may have noticed. The tic. His right eyelid twitching. Such a sweet man. Claudia and I think one of us shall have to take him under one's wing.'

They said their goodbyes.

'You will come again next month, won't you?' she said. 'In the summer, after the meeting, we all of us dance around the cherry tree in Claudia's back garden.'

That night as David lay in his bed, wearing his late wife's nightgown, and unable to sleep, he thought he heard in the distance low moaning sounds, as if from whales in distress calling to their kith and kin.

*

On the afternoon of the following day, David, wearing Joan's blue denim top, cropped pants, beneath a Jaeger pure wool full length coat, and black leather knee-high boots, walked to the boating lake, where, he had recently discovered from her diaries, Joan had visited from time to time on her own. The boating lake would seem to have been the place, as she wrote of it, where she had sought restoration.

David sat alone at a metal table beneath the awning of the boating lake café with his bought coffee and piece of apple pie. Wrapped up, as intended, against the December cold, he looked across the water, at the geese and seagulls, towards the low winter sun and up at the open sky.

Four mothers, each with their baby, their identical grey prams and pushchairs, were gathered about a table on the café's forefront. They came there, David guessed, most afternoons, their lives largely governed by repetition. They drank their coffees, their teas, held close their babies in their all-in-one pram suits, and now and then, as prompted, stood and gently jostled them to reassure.

The mothers began to pack away the feeding bottles. Off then to houses, to flats, who knows? To husbands or partners, or to no man or other at all. David, beneath the awning, could but wonder but he didn't expect to know.

A small boy in blue coat and scarf was dashing up and down the edge of the lake, scattering bread crumbs; first here, then further along, then back the other way again, excitedly, seagulls squawking, swooping, the geese arriving in stately procession. Clatter, clatter went the boy. Back he ran to his father for reinforcements. Up and down, he jumped.

The peddle-boats, eight feet tall plastic swans in white, red and green, out of commission on account of winter, were anchored 'out at sea', seagulls at rest on the tops of their guano-stained heads.

The sun sat low and fitfully across the water.

This was where they found her body.

IN THE BEGINNING

She looked at him and what she saw was his nose. It was large and red. She asked herself, what was a girl like her – fifty-three, but she didn't look it – doing on a date with a man who was well into his sixties? They were in the Batra Tandoori Restaurant off the High Street. He was seated across the table from her, tucking into his plate of Chicken Madras.

The man was no beauty. There was his nose, for a start. He was not obese as such. Not for his age. Men in their mid-to-late sixties had a thickening out.

He had grey hair that was thinning, and was brushed flat and had a wide parting on the left side. There were laugh lines about his eyes. She liked that. There was a sense of humour there, she told herself. Her name, she had told him, was Karen.

Behind her, formal against the predictable red-flock wallpaper, stood the middle-aged Indian waiter. He was wearing a black bow tie, clean white shirt, dark suit. What was he waiting for? she asked herself.

There were two glasses of red wine and a half empty bottle on the table. Merlot, she thought he said. Roses on the table, courtesy of the management. Also red. There were too many of them, and they were in danger of falling out of the vase.

She was on her second glass and the effect was upon her. Oh, all right, it was Friday. Who cared? And anyway, he was nice. He was gentlemanly. It was better than sitting at home on a Friday night. She knew after she had finished her second glass the man wouldn't be so bad. She'd been here before.

He was saying something. He held up the bottle.

'Oh, well,' she said.

He filled her glass. She was on her third.

He was nicely turned out, all things considered. He was wearing a suit in subtle tones of brown and grey. A white shirt and a brown tie. She couldn't make out if the suit was more brown than grey or the other way round. Was it just grey? Was it the red flock wallpaper that lent the suit the hint of brown?

She would have been able to see better if she had worn her glasses. They were attractive glasses, fake tortoiseshell. People had said they suited her. Only, she didn't like wearing them, not when she went out, not that evening.

Red flock wallpaper, she thought. Where else would one find wallpaper like that, other than in a Tandoori Restaurant off a High Street? It was not something one could have in one's living room A small piece of it in the loo perhaps, but that would be it.

The man sitting opposite her, helping himself to his Chicken Madras, had propositioned her in Tesco's. His name was Charlie. He had commented on her shopping, the macaroni and haddock bake in the wire basket. He had made her laugh. She couldn't remember what he had said that had made her laugh, but he had. He had said he liked to go for a curry on Fridays, and would she like to join him? And she had said, yes.

And there they were.

'I like it here,' he said. 'It's quiet.'

They were the only customers. A Friday night. July. The place, she thought, would close before the end of the year. It would be sold to another outfit, probably to another Indian, by Christmas.

That evening there had been two take-aways ordered. They were despatched by a young man wearing a crash helmet. His scooter was parked on the kerb outside in the dark night.

It was ten, coming up to ten-thirty.

She was on her third glass.

Earlier that evening after work, after she got back to her flat, she had showered.

She had chosen to wear her flowered navy-blue maxi dress, which covered her upper arms. It had cost her fifty-five quid.

She had brushed her abundant head of hair. It was a natural auburn even then at the age of fifty-three. Two weeks to go and she would be fifty-four. She had checked her smile. She had a great, friendly open smile. People, her 'girl-friends' at British Telecom where she worked, had said so. She pulled on the gold glitter sandals from Debenhams. She hung about her neck her yellow gold necklace.

She had had one final check of her smile in her living room mirror. Her teeth were her own if one didn't count the two crowns near the front. The picture was complete.

She was ready for Charlie and the Batra Tandoori off the High Street.

'I like it here,' he said.

Charlie was Clerk of Works for a building firm outside Havering. He liked the company of a woman at the end of the working week. On a Friday night, off he went to the Batra for a Madras Chicken, and, where possible, in the company of a pleasant woman. He had his desires. But he was respectful. Then on a Saturday morning it was the newsagent, the sports pages. And if they wanted to meet again, he wouldn't have said no.

The first woman he had brought to the Batra, a couple or so months back, had been a bit stiff, on the offensive. Hadn't liked the food and, after the coffee, she had phoned for a taxi to take her home.

The second had been drunk on arrival. She had wanted to know too much about him. His marriage. His wife. His wife's cancer. Her death. His job. His childhood in Eastbourne by the sea. There had been nothing left of him by the end of the evening.

Karen was more at ease, he thought. She sitting there with her Madras Chicken, same as himself. Lovely head of hair. She had it washed and cut once a month by Maggie at Harpers' Hair Stylists, she had told him. She took care of her appearance. Presented herself well. There was a bit of mischief about her. Very nice smile. She liked to laugh, that was for certain. He could make her laugh. Which was just as well, all things being considered. Laughter was the thing.

He had a nice voice, she thought; a London accent. It was unthreatening. She'd had enough of the other sort. She wasn't going back there. Her ex-husband had handed out enough of that. She hadn't told Charlie about her ex. Too early. It wasn't something she came up with on the first date, or the second, although it was 'a must' on the third. By the third, one had to lay it out, put the cards on the table. It had been her husband who had caused her to have the two crowns. It had been that that decided her to leave him. They'd not had kids. He went off and fathered two boys and a girl by another woman. Good luck to her, she had said. Thereafter, she had tried not to think of him.

She was on her third. Half way down the glass.

'Would you care for dessert? A brandy?' he said.

God no. Don't push it, Charlie.

A young Indian came into the restaurant from the kitchen. He stood by the counter as if to pass the time. Lean, tightly built. She would not have said no to him. Only, she couldn't imagine how she would deal with him before or after, or what they would have to say to each other.

The waiter at the red flock wallpaper had stepped forward.

'Everything all right?' he asked.

Charlie, his nose a brighter red and larger than it had been earlier in the evening, asked for the bill. The waiter had it in his hand. Charlie paid with his card.

She finished the third glass of red. The bottle was empty.

Charlie helped her on with her coat; a blue-and-white check with a fake fur collar.

'Thank you very much,' Charlie said to the waiter.

She stepped through the open door onto the pavement, Charlie, her Friday gentleman, ushering her ahead of him. It had started to drizzle. He put an arm around her shoulders. It was all right, she told herself. The fact was, one couldn't sit at home on one's own every evening, or one would never do anything or get anywhere.

The waiter cleared their table.

He went and stood by the cash till on the counter.

The lad from the kitchen had his jacket on. He had with him a carrier bag of food. He left.

The waiter turned the 'Open' sign on the door to 'Closed'.

The Essex Express and Herald. 14th June, 2022.
Mr Charles W. Morton and Miss Karen Wentworth.
The marriage took place on 10th June 2022 at the Church of St Laurence, Upminster.

Christopher Owen's stories have been published in a number of literary magazines and anthologies in the UK, USA, and Ireland. An Honourable Life won 1st prize for the Final Chapters Competition, and was republished in the Final Chapters anthology by Jessica Kingsley Publishers in 2014.

He won 2nd prize for the Wells Festival of Literature Short Story Competition 2019, and has been short-listed for the Bridport Story Prize 2019 and for the Hammond House Publishing Prize.

He has been long-listed for the Royal Society of Literature V. S. Pritchett Short Story Prize 2018, the Dorset Short Story Prize, and for the London Short Story Prize 2018.

His story *Cyril, Eyes Full of Drink* (in this Collection) has been Highly Commended (in top 5 of submissions) for THE COSTA SHORT STORY PRIZE 2021.

A Day At The Cricket (in this Collection) made the Top 50 from almost 1100 entries in the 2021 BBC National Short Story Award with Cambridge University.

His plays have been produced in the UK, Ireland, USA, Australia and the Gulf States. His play A Family Affair won 1st prize at the RAFTA Festival, Still Waters winner at the Lost Theatre Festival and played at the Manhattan Theatre Club, USA. Laying the Turf was long-listed for the Papatango New Writing Prize and by the Bush Theatre, London, 2018. The Touch of a Butterfly's Wing was long-listed for Papatango Award. 2016. In the 1990's he toured the UK and Gulf States with his shows A Parsons Tale and Right ho, Wodehouse!

He trained at RADA, and worked in theatre, television and film for over 50 years.

This book is printed on paper from sustainable sources managed under the Forest Stewardship Council (FSC) scheme.

It has been printed in the UK to reduce transportation miles and their impact upon the environment.

For every new title that Troubador publishes, we plant a tree to offset CO_2, partnering with the More Trees scheme.

MORE TREES
LET'S PLANT A BILLION TREES

For more about how Troubador offsets its environmental impact, see www.troubador.co.uk/sustainability-and-community